...this conversation. "What make...

"...ah." He gave her a look. "Don't even think ...t."

...hed in surrender. "Fine."

S... ...imply been stalling for time, anyway. Even if
s... ...nted to—which she didn't—there was no way
...convince Andrew he wasn't the father of this

... you going to tell me?"

...dded slowly. "Yes."

...n?"

front of Andrew, despite the nerves
quivering inside of her.

He rose as she approached. Bypassing a greeting,
Andrew went straight to the question she had expected.

"Why didn't you call me?"

She cleared her throat, wishing she'd prepared herself
somewhat better for this moment. "What makes
you think you...

THE TEXAN'S
SURPRISE BABY

BY
GINA WILKINS

...ion (UK) policy is to use papers that are natural, renewable and
...ble products and made from wood grown in sustainable forests. The
... and manufacturing processes conform to the legal environmental
...ons of the country of origin.

...ed and bound in Spain
... Litografia CPI, Barcelona

MILLS &
BOON

First published in Great Britain 2013
by Mills & Boon, an imprint of Harlequin (UK) Limited,
Eton House, 18-24 Paradise Road, Richmond, Surrey TW9 1SR

© Gina Wilkins 2013

ISBN: 978 0 263 90119 1
ebook ISBN: 978 1 472 00495 6

23-0613

Harlequi... recyclab...
logging a...
regulatio...

Printed a...
by Black...

Gina Wilkins is a bestselling and award-winning author who has written more than seventy novels for Mills & Boon. She credits her successful career in romance to her long, happy marriage and her three "extraordinary" children.

A lifelong resident of central Arkansas, Ms Wilkins sold her first book to Mills & Boon in 1988 and has been writing full-time since. She has appeared on the Waldenbooks, B. Dalton and *USA TODAY* bestseller lists. She is a three-time recipient of a Maggie Award for Excellence, sponsored by Georgia Romance Writers, and has won several awards from the reviewers of *RT Book Reviews*.

For my family, as always—
my wonderful husband, three extraordinary offspring,
amazing son-in-law and precious baby grandson.
There aren't enough adjectives to describe what
you all mean to me.

Prologue

"*Pregnant?*" Andrew Walker figured the hard thud in his abdomen was his heart falling straight into his stomach. "Hannah is expecting a baby?"

"Yeah. That was the first thing I noticed when I met her this morning after she came home from visiting her mother's relatives in Shreveport. I guess no one in the family thought to mention her condition to me before." His twin brother, Aaron, sounded a bit surprised by Andrew's apparent overreaction to a fleeting comment during an announcement-filled phone call.

"How, um, how is she?" Andrew asked, trying to wrap his mind around the news.

"Well, she nearly keeled over when I first saw her. Turned stark-white and swayed on her feet, scaring her family half to death. I thought she was startled by seeing me, for some reason, but it turned out she was just operating on very little sleep. Maybe a little dehydrated after a long drive."

Andrew's fingers had tightened so hard around the phone that he thought he heard the case groan in protest. "How, uh, how far along is she?"

His own uncharacteristic stammering annoyed him, but Aaron didn't seem to notice. "Shelby said she's due in mid-September, so about six months. I guess it's a surprise to you, because you haven't seen her in almost a year."

Six months. "Um. Right. And the father?"

"Not involved. No one really talks about it, but I got the impression this was sort of a one-time-thing accident, you know? Shelby told me it's totally out of character for Hannah, but the family figures she was still stinging after the fiasco with her ex-husband and indulged in a little ego boost that left her with unintended consequences. She's doing well, though, and everyone's excited about welcoming the first member of the new generation of Bells."

Not knowing what to say, Andrew just sort of grunted in response.

Aaron quickly changed the subject away from Bell family gossip. "Anyway, I just wanted to catch you up on what's been going on here. I hope you're happy for me."

Andrew hadn't been surprised to hear that Aaron had become seriously involved with a woman he'd known for only a matter of days. Even though he'd heard about Aaron's adventures with Shelby Bell only by telephone for the past week, there'd been something in his brother's voice that suggested Aaron had fallen hard and fast. Andrew had met Shelby the previous year and he could see how Aaron would be drawn to her. Apparently, the attraction had been immediate and mutual.

"Of course I'm happy for you," he said. "So you'll be staying at the resort?"

"Yes. Now that Shelby's brother is down with a broken leg, they need extra help here this summer. The opening will become permanent when he leaves in the fall to start his firefighter training. Because I'm looking for a new career anyway, I'd like to try working in a fishing-and-camping resort. So far the behind-the-scenes part of it has been fascinating."

"It's hard work. I saw that during the two weeks I spent with them."

"I've never been afraid of hard work. Just boredom. And I can't see myself getting bored here with Shelby and the rest of her family. I can understand why they have so many loyal returning guests. It's a great place for a getaway. A great place to make a home."

Andrew couldn't help thinking of his brother's so-far limited attention span, so restless that at only thirty Aaron had already experimented with maybe half a dozen careers. Andrew, on the other hand, had worked in the D'Alessandro-Walker Agency, their family's Dallas-based security and investigation business, from the time he was in high school and was now solidly entrenched to move into upper management when his father and uncles were ready to retire.

Through his job at the agency, he'd been hired by the Bell family almost a year ago to investigate a slick operator who'd been married to one of their own—Shelby's beautiful cousin, Hannah. The ex-husband had been in the process of trying to bankrupt the resort after Hannah divorced him. Andrew had found evidence that not only was Wade Cavender's legal posturing little more than a bogus extortion attempt, but he'd also been systematically stealing from the family for more than two years. Wade was now serving a too-short jail sentence for embezzlement. Andrew had thought he'd put his own complicated entanglement with the Bell family behind him—until his twin had stumbled upon a brochure for the Bell Resort and Marina in Andrew's office and had impulsively decided to take a vacation there.

Trying to focus on the conversation, Andrew pushed thoughts of Hannah to the back of his mind. Yet he knew those images would lurk there in the darkness, ready to taunt him again as soon as he let down his guard—just as thoughts of her had been doing for almost a year now. "Have you told Mom and Dad yet that you're staying there?"

"Just talked to Mom. Needless to say, she and Dad can't wait to meet Shelby. Shelby and I are planning a quick trip to Dallas soon to meet the folks and pick up some more of my things."

The Bell Resort was located on Lake Livingston, almost a four-hour drive south of Dallas. Aaron had planned to stay only a week or so, needing a chance to recharge and contemplate after leaving a job in which he'd been unhappy and unfulfilled. He couldn't have predicted then that he would find a new love, a new home and a new career there.

"How does Shelby's family feel about your moving in with her after knowing her only a week?"

"They're—" Aaron paused as if searching for a word, then finished with "—adjusting."

Aaron had saved Shelby's life the day before when she'd been attacked and kidnapped by a criminal who'd been using the resort as a base for his stolen-goods fencing operation. Shelby had stumbled onto the scheme and had a knife pressed to her throat as a result. Fortunately Aaron rescued her unharmed, which made him the newest Bell family hero. Still, it had to be unnerving for her parents and grandparents to see how quickly she and Aaron, who was little more than a stranger to them, had become lovers.

As for Andrew himself, well, when it came to the Bell women, he was in no position to judge.

"I'd better go," Aaron said. "Bryan's waiting for me to help him repair an outdoor light fixture. A couple of punk kids broke it by throwing rocks at it."

Aaron already sounded like an indignant resort property manager, Andrew noted. Had he not just been stunned by his brother's unwitting announcement, he might have found it rather amusing. As it was, he sat for a long time after disconnecting the call, staring blindly at his work-cluttered desk and wondering what the hell he was supposed to do now.

Chapter One

Hannah Bell figured she had a few days at the most to decide whether to run or stand her ground. She'd never considered herself a coward, but she was leaning toward running. She'd be leaving behind her loving, close-knit family, a marketing job she'd trained for all her life and her cozy manufactured home in the family owned Texas lake resort where she'd grown up. She would miss this tidy little two-bedroom trailer, the first place she'd ever lived that was hers alone.

Sitting in her neutral-toned living room, she sighed heavily, one hand on her swollen tummy as she silently conceded she wouldn't be going anywhere. As inviting as it sounded to disappear before the inevitable confrontation with Andrew Walker, she would stay and face the consequences of her own unprecedented behavior on one reckless winter night. It wouldn't do any good to run anyway. Andrew was a P.I. He'd find her if he wanted to.

Would he want to?

Four rapid knocks sounded on her front door—her sister Maggie's characteristic signal. "It's unlocked," she called out, too tired to rise.

Maggie entered carrying a plastic cup with a straw. It was almost five, so she was probably finished with her work for the day. Maggie had chosen the job of house-keeping supervisor, hiring and overseeing the cleaning staff for the sixteen-unit motel and eight cabins available for rent in the resort. Having majored in business and Spanish in college, Maggie performed her job efficiently and cheerfully. She kept her employees on task and held them to high standards of cleanliness and customer service, yet they still liked her and would gladly do anything she asked. Hannah had always been impressed with her sister's easy people skills. Even though she worked closely with the public herself in her role as marketing and scheduling supervisor for the resort, along with manning the front desk for check-ins, she was more naturally reserved and had to put a little more effort into her interactions.

"I brought you a strawberry smoothie," Maggie said. "I figured you could use an energy boost."

Hannah accepted the cup gratefully. "Thanks, sis."

"You're welcome. So, big news about Shelby and Aaron Walker, huh?"

Swallowing a gulp of the cold, fruity beverage, Hannah nodded, giving herself a moment to choose her words before answering. "I was shocked to hear Shelby's gotten involved with Aaron Walker. But, then, I didn't even know Andrew's brother was here."

Having been out of the state for a couple of weeks visiting their mother's relatives in Shreveport, Hannah had missed the recent excitement here at Bell Resort and Marina, a business her family had owned for three generations. Her impetuous and imaginative cousin Shelby had suspected that a man renting one of the vacation cabins was involved in something illegal and had found herself in danger when she'd been proven right. Hannah shuddered to think of the knife that had been held to Shelby's throat only the day before. Maggie had told her all about the nightmarish scene and about Aaron's daring rescue of their cousin. Shelby sported an ugly bruise on one cheek from the ordeal.

Hannah would bet it would be a while before the family recovered from that shock, especially right on the heels of Shelby's older brother Steven's accident. He'd broken his leg and suffered a concussion when he'd overturned a mowing tractor while working around the campgrounds. Two near-tragedies in less than a week had been hard on their grandparents, not to mention Steven and Shelby's parents. The family needed a few days of peace and comfortable routines.

Hannah was going to do her best to keep from upsetting them for a while. She had shocked them enough when she'd announced her pregnancy a couple months ago when it had started to become obvious. Now six months along, she still refused to name the father. She had let them believe her condition was the result of an impulsive and completely uncharacteristic one-night stand, which was true, with someone they didn't know, which was not exactly accurate. She had made it quite clear that she wanted this child, that while her pregnancy might have been an accident, she would never label it a mistake. And bless their hearts, her family had rallied around her. She had no doubt they would welcome the newest member of their family with love and joy.

Sitting in a chair with the bottled water she'd brought for herself, Maggie brushed back her sun-streaked brown hair and studied Hannah with long-lashed hazel eyes. Hannah's hair was a darker brown than her sister's and her eyes were emerald-green. They would never be mistaken for twins, but she knew there were family resemblances between them, from their mother's coloring to their father's cheekbones.

"So, how are you feeling?" Maggie asked. "You looked pretty shaky when you arrived this morning."

"That was probably too long a drive to make without more breaks," Hannah admitted. "I thought leaving Grammy's house at dawn to avoid the heat of the day was a good idea, but maybe I should have slept in a little longer."

"You're going to have to take better care of yourself," Maggie fussed. "Eat better, get more rest. You can't just—" She stopped with a laugh. "Oh, gosh, I sound like Mom, don't I?"

Hannah smiled. "You do, but thanks for the concern anyway. I'll be more careful."

"You have a doctor's appointment this week?"

"Yes, Friday. I'm having an ultrasound, so maybe this time I'll finally see if it's a boy or a girl." She was eager to know the sex, but the little peanut hadn't cooperated by getting into the right position during her earlier scan. Her ob-gyn had assured her they would probably know by the end of the upcoming visit.

Maggie grinned. "I can't wait to find out if I'm having a niece or a nephew. I'm going to be the coolest aunt ever."

Hannah laughed. "I have no doubt."

Sobering, Maggie set her water bottle aside. "You should probably tell your doctor you almost fainted this morning. Your face went so white it scared me."

Hannah concentrated on stirring her smoothie with the plastic straw. "Like I said, I was just tired."

She had no intention of admitting that the unexpected sight of Aaron Walker standing with the rest of her family in the resort diner had drained all the blood from her head. For a heart-stopping moment, she'd mistaken him for his identical twin. She'd thought Andrew was there to see her, and a dozen panicked questions had flashed through her mind—most notably, had he somehow found out about the pregnancy?

Aaron had reached out to steady her when she'd swayed, and she'd realized almost instantly that he wasn't Andrew. Even had he not worn his dark coffee-colored hair longer than his brother, she'd have known the truth with one look at his face. There was something in his eyes that was fundamentally different from Andrew's, something she couldn't quite define but recognized nonetheless. She couldn't say she remembered much more about that meeting with Aaron, other than to make note that Aaron and Shelby had just announced they were a couple and that Aaron would be staying to work in the resort. Which meant it was inevitable that Andrew would eventually visit again to see his brother.

She rested a hand on her stomach, feeling the baby do a lazy turn inside.

"Have you decided on names yet?" Maggie asked.

"Not yet. I'll wait until I know the sex."

Maggie slipped in one more question in the same chatty tone. "Told the dad yet?"

Hannah gave her a look. While the rest of the family had accepted her refusal to discuss the matter, her younger sister didn't give up so easily. "No."

"Going to?"

"Yes." She had always planned to do so eventually, though she'd yet to decide how or when. She'd thought she had two or three more months to figure it out. Now it seemed her time was up.

As if in confirmation of that acknowledgment, her cell phone chirped to announce a text message. She checked it warily, and was not as surprised as she probably should have been to see the sender's name.

"I have to run to town for a little while," she said, setting her half-empty smoothie cup aside.

Maggie blinked in surprise. "I thought you were going to rest this afternoon."

"I've rested all day. There are some things I need to do now because I plan to be back at my desk first thing in the morning."

Looking concerned, Maggie rose as Hannah did. "Do you want me to come with you?"

"No, thanks. I won't be long." At least she hoped not.

"Hannah—"

She rested a hand on Maggie's arm. "I'm okay," she said, trying to sound reassuring. "There's just something I need to see to, okay?"

"You'll let me know if you need me?"

"You know I will."

Even though Maggie didn't look happy about it, she let her go. Hannah drew a deep breath for courage as she headed for the door.

* * *

The public boat launch was set on a cove a fifteen-minute drive away from the Bell Resort and Marina. Shaded by tall leafy trees, it consisted of little more than the launch ramp, a parking lot and a few picnic tables. The place was nearly deserted on this Monday afternoon in mid-June, though a couple of parked trucks with empty boat trailers attached indicated fishermen would return later. A dark gray sports car looked out of place among the pickup-and-trailer combos.

Parking her own sensible little sedan, Hannah glanced through the windshield at the dark-haired, dark-eyed man who was watching her gravely from one of the picnic tables. He sat backward on the bench, facing the parking lot, his long legs stretched out in front of him. Wearing a blue polo shirt and jeans, Andrew Walker looked casual and relaxed, as though he had nothing more on his mind than an appreciation of the warm, cloudless afternoon. Hannah knew that impression was deceptive.

It wasn't their first time to meet alone here. They'd come here to talk when he'd worked for her family early last August, trying to help them clean up the mess her ex-husband—now known in the family as "the evil ex"—had deliberately created. It wasn't easy finding privacy among her ever-present family at the resort, so she'd brought Andrew here one afternoon to discuss the case frankly, telling him things about her failed marriage she hadn't confided even to her relatives. She'd ended up sobbing into his shoulder, a memory that still made her cringe with embarrassment, but he'd been so kind and understanding that she'd probably fallen a little in love with him that very afternoon. She'd done her best to hide her feelings for him—feelings she neither trusted nor expected to lead anywhere—until that momentous, wholly unexpected night in December.

She couldn't keep procrastinating getting out of her car. She refused to look like a coward in front of Andrew, despite the nerves quivering inside of her. Chin held high, she opened her door and climbed out. She hadn't gained much weight so far during her pregnancy. Her sister teased her that it looked as though she had a basketball tucked beneath her shirt because the rest of her body was pretty much unchanged. Giving one self-conscious tug to the peasant-styled yellow top she wore with drawstring white cotton pants, she walked toward Andrew.

He rose as she approached. To give him credit, his gaze focused on her face, not her tummy. He wore his dark coffee-colored hair short, neatly trimmed, brushed off his clean-shaven face. His eyes were almost black. His jaw was firm, his nose straight, lips beautifully shaped, though stern now. He was still the best-looking man she'd ever known—though of course, Aaron looked exactly like him with the exception of a longer hairstyle. Yet looking at Aaron that morning, she'd instantly decided Andrew was still the more handsome—a ridiculous fancy, even though she held that same belief now.

Bypassing a greeting, Andrew went straight to the question she had expected. "Why didn't you call me?"

She cleared her throat, wishing she'd prepared herself somewhat better for this conversation. "What makes you think you're—"

"Hannah—" he gave her a look "—don't even think about it."

She sighed in surrender. "Fine."

She'd simply been stalling for time anyway. Even if she wanted to—which she didn't—there was no way she'd convince Andrew he wasn't the father of this baby. He could count on his fingers as well as any guy. And even though they'd spent only a few short weeks in each other's company during the ten months since they'd met, he'd gotten to know her well enough that he would have no doubt that night with him had been an anomaly for her.

"Were you going to tell me?"

She nodded slowly. "Yes."

"When?"

"Soon. I just—" She paused, then shrugged. "I didn't know what to say."

Both his voice and his expression softened in response to her helpless tone. "I can understand that."

She clasped her hands in front of her and looked down at them, unable to meet Andrew's eyes just then.

His hands were gentle when they fell on her shoulders, but still her pulse raced in response to his touch. "Are you okay? You haven't had any problems?"

She shook her head. "I'm in perfect health. And so is the baby."

His gaze lowered then, focusing on her middle. He cleared his throat. "Is it—do you know if it's a boy or a girl?"

"I'll find out Friday."

His eyes rose and she saw the emotions he'd concealed to this point. She had learned during their one night together that the rather stoic control Andrew usually displayed masked an intense, passionate nature. Memories of that passion made her catch her breath, her heart thudding hard against her chest. A muscle flexed in Andrew's jaw and the slightest tremor moved his fingers against her shoulders, making her suspect the same images were flashing through his mind. She felt her cheeks warm in a way that had nothing to do with the hot afternoon temperature.

Andrew dropped his hands a little too abruptly, shoving them into his pockets. By unspoken agreement, they both shifted to put another couple of inches between them.

"Have you told your family? About me?" he clarified.

She shook her head. "They have no idea. I never even told them I saw you in Dallas in December."

"I see."

So much of that fateful evening had hinged on impulse. She'd been in Dallas for an annual holiday gathering with some college friends, and had dropped by Andrew's office with the excuse of giving him an update about her ex-husband's sentencing—which he'd already known, having kept up with the case. He'd politely asked her to dinner and they'd had drinks at her hotel afterward. One thing had led to another, and then...

Automatically, she rested a hand on her stomach.

"I guess Aaron told you I was pregnant." She'd known that was inevitable from the moment she'd seen Aaron with Shelby.

Andrew nodded. "It slipped into our conversation earlier today. Needless to say, it threw me for a loop. I— well, I guess the precautions we took that night weren't enough. I know there's always a chance, but still..."

The awkwardness was unlike him, merely another sign of how shaken he'd been. "You didn't say anything to Aaron about—"

He quickly shook his head. "I just threw some things in a bag and headed this way."

Normally it was a four-hour drive from Dallas to the resort. Hannah suspected Andrew had made it in less today.

She twisted her fingers more tightly together. "You're coming to the resort?"

"Yes."

"Would you—could we not say anything to the family just yet? About your being the father, I mean. We'll tell them," she added quickly, when he started to frown, "just not until we've had more time to talk privately about…things."

To her relief, he nodded to concede that she had a valid point. "We will need to talk."

"Yes." And she dreaded it. Everything was so complicated. "But it's going to take a while. And I can't do it now, the family will be wondering where I am. The way I rushed off without an explanation, they'll be worried if I don't go back soon."

He didn't look particularly pleased with the delay, but he didn't try to argue. "So how are we playing this?"

"We'll show up at the resort at different times so they won't know we've already seen each other. You can go ahead, I need to stop by the store anyway."

"And I suppose you'll be completely surprised to find me at the resort when you get back."

She shrugged, intending to play it exactly that way.

Andrew sighed and ran a hand over his hair. "Fine. We'll do it your way. I'll keep your secret. For now. But somehow or another we'll have to find opportunities to talk, and soon."

She nodded grimly, knowing his patience would last only so long. "We'll talk."

She turned toward her car, only to be stopped by his hand on her arm. "Hannah."

Looking up at him, she whispered, "What?"

"It's going to be okay."

She moistened her lips. "I know."

He smoothed a strand of hair away from her cheek. "I'll see you at the resort."

Nodding, she hurried toward her car, resisting an impulse to lay a hand on her cheek where his fingers had touched.

She drove straight to the grocery store. She had forgotten to bring a list and she was still so rattled from her brief meeting with Andrew that she could hardly think about what she needed. She drifted down the aisles of the store fifteen minutes after parting from him, staring blankly at the shelves and trying to focus on the task at hand rather than the challenges that lay ahead. With yogurt, fresh fruit and a bag of cookies in her cart, she turned a corner only to have her day take yet another downturn as she came face-to-face with her former in-laws, Justine and Chuck Cavender. It was the first time she had seen them since their son had been arrested for embezzlement and attempted extortion against Hannah's family.

"Hannah!" Justine's first startled reaction was pleasure. She and Hannah had gotten along well enough before the acrimonious divorce. But then her gaze lowered and her smile was replaced with a stricken expression. "Oh. You're—"

Chuck had never been particularly fond of Hannah to start with—primarily, Hannah suspected, because he'd believed every lie Wade had told about what a terrible wife she'd been. Chuck had enabled, apologized for and deflected blame for his son for all of Wade's life, which Hannah believed was part of the reason Wade sat in jail now. Wade could be charming, convincing and manipulative—her marriage to him was proof enough of that—but the streak of meanness that lay beneath his amiable mask came straight from his father.

Chuck snarled at Hannah, "Get out of our way."

She scooted her cart as far to one side as she could. She almost apologized for being in his path, but she bit her tongue. She'd apologized too many times to both Wade and his father for things that had not been her fault. She was not sliding back into that pattern now. Chuck shoved his cart forward, almost slamming into hers despite the room she had left him.

Falling into step behind her husband, Justine gave Hannah a mournful look. "I'd always hoped you and Wade would give us grandchildren," she murmured.

"Instead, she sent our boy to prison," Chuck snapped over his shoulder, discounting Wade's part in his fate. "And then went slutting around and got herself knocked up when she's not even married. Personally, I'm glad she isn't a mother to any grandchildren of ours."

Miserably aware of a few gawkers within hearing range, Hannah held her chin high with an effort, moved toward the front of the store with her few purchases, paid as quickly as possible and left with as much dignity as she could scrape together. Her day had gone from bad to worse, but maybe she had needed that awful encounter. It would serve as a painful reminder that her track record with men was not good.

In the past, she'd seen what she wanted to see, trusted

when she shouldn't have, believed when she should have delved more deeply. She wasn't that naive, sheltered, starry-eyed girl now. Nor was she the lonely, vulnerable woman who'd been swept into a reckless night of passion by a sexy smile and a gleaming pair of dark eyes. She knew now who she was, where she belonged and what she wanted—and she would do well to keep those things in mind during the coming days.

At half past six, the day was still sunny and warm, the sprawling blue lake still busy with boaters, skiers and swimmers. This time of year, the resort would bustle every day of the week with families taking vacations from jobs and school, and the Bell family would be kept hopping, though Andrew hadn't heard them complain during the two weeks he'd spent here last summer. With the exception of Shelby's brother, Steven, they all seemed to love the jobs they'd chosen. Steven had grown restless and would be leaving soon to try his hand at his boyhood dream of firefighting, but Andrew figured there was a chance he'd be back someday to take his place in the family business.

After passing through the manned entry gate, he took a right on the circular main road through the resort. A two-story lakeside building held the reception office, convenience store and diner, with the private business offices upstairs, and the marina at the back. He parked in front and climbed out of his car. To his right lay the public swimming pool, the sixteen-room lakeside motel and three of the eight cabins. Turning left, he saw the pavilion and playground often occupied by family reunions, corporate gatherings or other events. Beyond the pavilion lay the day-use area, five more stand-alone cabins, RV pads with hookups and tent camping grounds.

A steady stream of resort guests flowed both ways through the big double glass doors, some in swimwear and cover-ups, most in shorts and tank tops or T-shirts, some carrying bags of purchases as they exited. The marina, store and grill would be open until seven, and Andrew figured the diner would be full now with customers hungry after a day of water sports. The air carried whiffs of boat motor exhaust from the lake and burning charcoal from the campgrounds, scents that had become very familiar to him during his almost-two-week stay last summer.

He still remembered the first time he'd entered this building after having been hired by the family last year. That was the day he'd met Hannah, who was twenty-seven then, the eldest of the Bell cousins by a few months. Chagrined that her ex-husband had caused her family so much trouble and anxiety, she'd held her chin high, her emerald eyes glittering with anger and determination. Andrew had taken one look at her and almost swallowed his tongue, his first thought being that she was the most beautiful woman he'd ever seen.

He'd managed to keep his distance from her for the most part during the next two weeks only by constantly reminding himself that he was on a job, and that it would be unprofessional of him to get involved with a client. He'd told himself she was too vulnerable, having been so recently divorced and dealing with the painful repercussions of her unfortunate choice of a spouse. They had been surrounded almost constantly by her caring and inquisitive family. Not to mention that he and Hannah had seemed an unlikely couple, with both of them committed to family businesses four hours apart, and with her announcing to all and sundry that she had no intention of getting married or even seriously involved with anyone again for a long time, if ever. Not even thirty himself then, he'd thought that sounded like a wise plan.

And then she'd shown up at his office in December, and he'd foolishly decided he'd been given an early Christmas gift. Maybe the holiday should have been April Fool's Day instead, considering the situation he found himself in now.

"Hey, Aaron. What are you doing standing out here in a daze? Come on inside and—wait." Maggie Bell skidded to a stop on the pavement nearby, studying him with a frown. "Okay, either you've cut your hair in the past hour or you aren't Aaron. Andrew?"

He smiled at her. "Hello, Maggie. Nice to see you again."

"Wow." She shook her head, tucking a strand of silky brown hair behind her left ear. "Now that I've spent a few days with your brother, it's even more startling that you look so exactly alike. I'm sure you get tired of hearing that."

He shrugged good-naturedly. "Part of the identical-twins thing. We don't mind."

"We didn't even know you had an identical twin until Aaron showed up here," she pointed out. "I'm not sure Pop believes even now that there are two of you."

He chuckled. Having met her unconventional grandfather, he wasn't surprised. The man everyone, even those who weren't related, called Pop was renowned for both his practical jokes and his twisted logic, making it hard to tell when he was kidding and when he was serious. "Maybe he'll believe it when he sees us standing side by side."

Maggie looped a hand beneath his arm and laughed as she led him toward the door. "I wouldn't even bet on that. Come on in, I'm sure we'll find some of the family in the grill at this hour."

Big double glass doors led into the main building. Stepping out of the hot summer day into the air-conditioned lobby, Andrew noted that nothing had changed since he'd last been here. Colorful mounted fish and antique lures displayed on wooden plaques decorated the walls, and lush greenery brought a touch of the outdoors inside. The reception desk faced the entrance, with the private upstairs offices accessible by a stairway and elevator behind the desk.

The Chimes Grill, decorated in retro '50s red vinyl and chrome, opened to the right of the entryway of the building. As he'd expected, he saw that the diner was busy, most of the tables and bar stools filled with customers. Opposite the grill, a small convenience store was lined with shelves of groceries, souvenirs and camping and fishing supplies. At the back of the building lay the marina, where C. J. Bell—father to Steven, Shelby and Lori—sold bait, fuel, motor oil and other marine supplies; rented out fishing boats, ski boats, pontoon boats and personal watercraft; and kept an eye on the boat slips and fishing pier. Part-time employees helped the family with the various aspects of the resort, but the Bells were most definitely in charge, the responsibilities divided by personal interests.

Shelby's younger sister Lori manned the reception desk at the moment. Andrew remembered her as being somewhat offbeat, with a penchant for trendy haircuts and colors and floaty smoke-colored clothing. Her hair was shaped in an asymmetrical wedge now, dyed black with bright blue streaks, and her clothes were charcoal-and dove-gray, proving her tastes hadn't changed since he'd last seen her. She looked surprised when Maggie led him in, her dark-lined eyes darting from him to the diner and then back again, making him suspect his brother was inside.

"Look who's here," Maggie said. "It's Andrew."

Andrew would have stopped then to check for an availability in the motel, but Maggie almost dragged him into the diner before he and Lori had time to do much more than exchange nods of greeting.

"There's your brother," Maggie said, pointing to a table at the far side of the room. "I thought he might be in here. He usually comes in after work for a cold iced tea or lemonade before dinner."

Aaron sat at a big table with Shelby, her brother, their uncle and Maggie's father, Bryan Bell, and the oldest members of the Bell clan, "Pop" and "Mimi." Shelby's mother, Sarah, worked the grill. Her dad, C.J., was probably still back at the marina, which was his personal domain. Andrew suspected some of the others had offered to help Sarah, but as he recalled, she was as proprietary about her work space as the others were with their chosen roles. She kept the menu simple and limited so she could handle the demand herself under most circumstances.

Aaron spotted Andrew and Maggie before the others did. His eyebrows rose in surprise as he gave a little salute of recognition, making the others turn to look. Andrew was inundated with a babble of excited greetings, drawn to the table for a barrage of questions and welcomes.

"Would you look at the two of you standing side by side," Mimi marveled with a shake of her silver head when Aaron rose to greet him. "I could tell you apart, of course, even if your hair was the same because I have a knack for that sort of thing, but I'm sure most people would have a difficult time."

Blonde, curly-haired, blue-eyed and girl-next-door-cute, Shelby wrinkled her nose in response to her grandmother's unlikely boast, sharing a smile with Aaron before holding out her right hand to Andrew. The hand-shaped bruise on her cheek was a solemn reminder of the ordeal she had survived. Andrew felt a wave of fury at the thought of someone hitting her; he could only imagine how his brother must feel every time he saw that mark.

"It's good to see you," she said, her characteristically cheerful spirit not notably dampened. "Did Aaron tell you I gave him a big hug the first time I saw him, thinking he was you?"

"No, he didn't," he replied with a laugh, tugging at her hand. "But I'll take my hug now."

She embraced him warmly, then stepped back with slightly narrowed eyes, though she was still smiling. "Okay, fess up. Did you come to make sure I'm not holding your brother hostage or anything? I know he told you this morning that he and I are together now, and suddenly here you are. Have you come to steal him away from me?"

"Why would I do that? I consider my brother to be a very lucky man."

She dimpled. "That's sweet. Thank you."

He squeezed her hand, then released her and nodded toward his brother. "I decided you had the right idea about taking a few days to relax here."

Aaron's brows shot even higher. "You were able to just take off from work on such short notice? I thought your calendar was so full for the rest of the year that you didn't have time to breathe, much less disappear on impulse like this."

"I just had to rearrange a couple of things." Like heaven and earth. His poor administrative assistant had been forced to move both to free the rest of the week at Andrew's request. His dad and uncles weren't exactly happy about his decision either, because they had to pick up the slack. They probably thought he'd come to make sure Aaron wasn't being foolishly impulsive, so it was likely their father secretly approved of the mission. Andrew couldn't imagine what everyone would say when they found out the real reason for the unscheduled trip.

"Can I get you a cold drink, Andrew?" Sarah called from behind the counter. She hadn't changed a bit since the last time he'd seen her, looking little older than her adult offspring. Her blond hair was just sprinkled with gray, her minimally made-up face was hardly lined, and while she carried a few extra pounds, she still looked fit and healthy.

"A lemonade sounds great," he answered with a smile, fondly remembering the fresh-squeezed lemonade he'd enjoyed last summer.

"I'll get it." Shelby hurried toward the counter.

Sandy-haired, blue-eyed, twenty-seven-year-old Steven Bell held out his right hand. "I'd stand to greet you, but I'm still sort of clumsy with these damn crutches," he complained.

Andrew shook his hand. "I was sorry to hear about your accident. How are you holding up, Steven?"

"Not bad, thanks. The leg should be completely healed in a few weeks with no lasting problems. The rest of me is still sore but better. All in all, could be worse."

"Aaron told me you're planning to train as a fire-fighter."

"Yeah, I'm hoping to start training as soon as I'm out of this cast. Fire and EMT classes start in mid-October, so I want to be in top shape by then."

"Well, Dad?" Hannah's father asked Pop with a grin. "Now do you believe there really are two of them?"

Pop chuckled. "Always did. I was just pulling Aaron's leg by pretending otherwise."

"How long can you be with us, Andrew?" Mimi asked eagerly, still avidly studying him and his brother as if searching for any minute difference.

"I'm not sure yet," he prevaricated. "Through the end of the weekend probably, unless something comes up."

"Where would you like to stay? Cabin 7 is available now," she said blithely. "And I guess Cabin 8 is open, too, if your brother is going to be shacking up with my granddaughter."

Andrew heard a few gasps and muffled laughs.

"Mother!" Bryan chided in a strangled voice.

"What?" Mimi looked from one of her family members to another with a matter-of-fact shrug. "We're a modern family. We're down with it."

This time it was Andrew who choked on a laugh.

"Oh, man, Mimi's been watching old sitcom reruns again," Steven said with an affectionate groan.

"One of the motel rooms will be fine with me, if it's available," Andrew assured them. "I don't need to tie up a cabin because I probably won't use the kitchen anyway. I don't cook much."

Mimi nodded. "We have a couple empty rooms. I think the one you stayed in last summer is available."

"That would be great. I enjoyed the view of the lake from the balcony."

She stood. "Here, take my seat. I have to go. The family's gathering at our house after closing for white chicken chili that's been cooking in Crock-Pots all day, and I have a few things to finish up. We'd love for you to join us."

"It would be my pleasure. Thank you."

She patted his cheek as though he were ten rather than thirty. "I'll have Lori bring you a key to your room. It's almost time for her to close the desk. She's on her summer break from college and she's been filling in for Hannah during the past couple weeks while Hannah visited some relatives."

Towing Pop along with her with the firm reminder that she required his assistance with dinner preparations, Mimi swept out of the diner. Andrew took her emptied seat, with his lemonade on the table in front of him. He glanced at his watch. Still another twenty minutes to go before the seven-o'clock closing time. After that, late arrivals wanting a room or campsite would have to ring a bell at the gate for service. One of the family members was always on call to answer that kind of summons, night duty rotating among the various households.

They spent those remaining twenty minutes talking— though more accurately, Andrew primarily listened, having little chance to get a word in with Shelby, Maggie, Steven and Bryan talking over each other to catch him up on what he'd missed. They told him more about the excitement yesterday with stolen-goods fencer Russell King, aka Terrence Landon, who had used Cabin 7 as his own private base of criminal operations for almost a month before Shelby and Aaron shut him down. The conversation segued into all the maintenance tasks scheduled for the remainder of the summer and beyond—chores that had been on Steven's agenda before his mowing accident and subsequent decision to pursue his childhood dream. Now Aaron was excited about taking over Steven's job with Bryan, who would be his direct supervisor.

Andrew watched his brother's face while the men talked about those upcoming projects. The work would be hard, mostly manual labor in the summer heat, but Aaron looked as though he couldn't wait to get started. He hadn't shown nearly as much enthusiasm for his last couple of jobs, both in sales with comfortable working conditions and a more-than-adequate income. Who'd have thought he'd get this stimulated working in resort maintenance? How much of his eagerness had to do with his new and exciting relationship with Shelby? Would it last or would it fall apart with time, leaving everyone involved disappointed and heartbroken?

Andrew had no precognitive talent, but he wanted to believe his brother would make his new direction in both romance and career work for a lifetime. Their family had a history of short courtships and long marriages, so maybe Aaron had inherited that gene.

As for himself—

"Oh, look, Hannah's back," Shelby said, waving toward the doorway behind Andrew. "She'll be so happy you're here, Andrew."

Hoping his smile didn't look as sickly as it felt, Andrew nodded, taking a moment to steel himself for the performance ahead. He sensed his brother studying him a bit too closely—or was that just projection on his part? Avoiding Aaron's eyes, he glanced in Maggie's direction, only to find her looking at him with a slight frown.

Clearing his throat, he stood and turned to watch Hannah approach, a credible expression of pleased surprise on her face when she saw him there. Pasting on a bright grin, he stepped forward. "Hello, Hannah. It's a pleasure to see you again."

Chapter Two

Even though nearly everyone had private quarters, the Bell clan often gathered at the end of a workday for meals. The family compound lay on a clearly marked private drive off the main resort road. Three almost-identical redbrick ranch-style houses were occupied by Hannah's grandparents, her parents and her aunt and uncle, with her grandparents in the center. As the third generation had become adults, they'd chafed against living with their parents and invested in homes of their own at the end of the road. Four similar tan-and-cream, two-bedroom mobile homes were grouped two on either side of the dead-end drive. Their grandfather grumpily referred to the tidy cluster as the "trailer park," but Hannah and her sister and cousins had been content with their quarters. Lori was the only one of their generation who still lived with her parents, though for most of the year she was away at college.

Mimi and Pop were the hosts on this Monday evening, and everyone was there except Lori, who had a
date, much to the displeasure of her family. While Hannah was away, it had come to light that Lori's current
boyfriend was Zach Webber, a long-haired, bearded
rebel who had dropped out of college and was currently
scraping by as a guitarist in an alternative garage band.
Maybe the family could have accepted all of that, Hannah mused, had they not known he'd done time in juvenile detention for breaking and entering. Probably his
legal records were sealed now that he was twenty-one,
but Zach had long been the subject of local gossip and
tongue-clucking and the family was not at all happy
that Lori had chosen to stage a mini-rebellion with him.

The topic of the evening was still the excitement of
the day before, though Shelby soon got tired of rehash-
ing it and begged everyone to talk about something
else. Grouped around the two large picnic tables that
sat behind her grandparents' house, the family obliged,
several new conversations breaking out at once among
the twelve diners enjoying Mimi's white chicken chili
and jalapeño corn muffins. Steven's lazy yellow lab,
Pax, wandered around the tables, not exactly begging
but giving longing looks to everyone with a plate. With
amusement, Hannah saw several members of the family
slipping bits of chicken to the dog even though Steven
expressly forbade them to do so.

Obsessed as always with work, Hannah's father
spoke up above the chatter, directing his words toward
Aaron. "You know anything about running electrical
wiring?"

"I'm not a licensed electrician, but I've helped with
a few basic projects. Why?"

"I'm wanting to install a few more security lights along our private drive, especially there around the sign," Hannah's dad said gruffly. His meaningful glance at Shelby made it clear that he was thinking of the one short, dark stretch on the drive where Shelby had been snatched while walking home late from visiting Aaron's cabin. None of them knew if more lighting would have prevented the attack, but maybe she'd have seen him lurking there had the shadows not been so heavy.

Aaron nodded approvingly, reaching out to cover Shelby's hand with his in a sweet, loving gesture that made Hannah's throat tighten for some reason. "I think I can help with that," Aaron said.

"Oh, by the way, Hannah," Mimi called out from the next table. "I saw Jenny Malone at church yesterday. She wants to host a baby shower for you. We're thinking maybe in about six weeks, which will give you time to prepare a list of guests you want her to invite and to register for gifts."

Hannah felt her face warm in response to having everyone's attention turned to her—one person's in particular. "That's very sweet of her," she murmured, "but not necessary. I really don't need a baby shower."

"Of course you do," Mimi insisted with a firm bob of her head. "Just because you're an unwed mother doesn't mean you won't need baby supplies. And your friends will want to do this for you."

If Hannah could have slid beneath the table gracefully, she would have done so then. She looked quickly to her sister for help, hoping Maggie would get the message to change the subject.

"Hannah's going to be a wonderful mother," Mimi

said in Andrew's direction before anyone could say anything. "We're all very excited about the baby."

Andrew glanced at Hannah briefly before responding to the older woman. "I'm sure you are."

Looking archly at Shelby and Aaron, Mimi added, "You know, Andrew, even though Hannah's expecting, she isn't involved with anyone at the moment."

Hannah choked on a sip of iced tea.

Mercifully, Maggie stepped in. "Mimi, I forgot to tell you that I saw Esther Lincoln in town Saturday. She said to be sure to tell you hello."

Predictably, their grandmother bristled at the name of her old archenemy, thoughts of matchmaking abruptly forgotten. "I'll just bet she did. She knew it would remind me of her and her scheming ways which she figured would ruin my day. Well, I just won't let it."

"Esther and Mimi competed in bake-offs at the county fair when they were younger," Hannah heard Shelby explain in a low voice to Aaron and Andrew. "It was not a friendly competition."

"Because she cheated in every which way she could, from kissing up to the judges to using recipes she found in the Julia Child cookbooks," Mimi retorted indignantly, proving there was nothing wrong with her hearing.

"Now, Mom, don't get started on that again." Hannah's uncle C.J. changed the subject to tell a funny story about a quirky customer he'd served at the marina that afternoon, which led to other anecdotes for Aaron and Andrew's benefit. Everyone laughed at the appropriate times, but Hannah could see that her grandmother still fumed about her old grievances and her aunt Sarah kept looking at the empty space where Lori usually sat.

Andrew's chuckles sounded a bit strained—understandably. She figured her own smiles would look forced to anyone studying her too closely, but she was fairly confident she was getting away with them for now.

She was going to have a firm talk with her grandmother later. This situation was difficult enough; it would be untenable if Mimi decided to try matchmaking between Hannah and Andrew while he was here. Mimi meant well of course, and she had no idea Andrew was the father of Hannah's baby. Once she found out the truth, the pressure would intensify. If there was one overwhelming thing Hannah did not want, it was for Andrew to feel obligated to propose to her just because her family—or his, for that matter—expected him to do so. The very idea depressed her.

Even though the family usually sat around chatting after meals, Hannah didn't linger long. She helped clear away, then claimed weariness, having started that day much too early. Her sister walked her home.

"Thanks for the rescue during dinner, Maggie," Hannah said when they reached her door.

Maggie chuckled ruefully. "You're welcome. I saw the look Mom shot at Mimi. I'm sure she'll ask her not to make future gatherings so awkward for you."

"I hope so."

Laughing a little, Maggie shook her head. "You have to give Mimi credit for nerve. She's determined to find you a husband. Could she have been any more blatant about trying to fix you up with Andrew?"

"I thought I was going to slide right under the table."

Maggie patted her arm. "I'm sure you did, but you have to admit Mimi has good taste. Andrew's a catch."

Hannah shot a frown at her sister. "You aren't suggesting—"

Maggie held up both hands in a quick gesture of surrender. "No agenda at all here. Just saying. It seemed like there was a little chemistry between you last year."

"Chemistry? You mean when he was helping us stop my jerk of an ex-husband from bankrupting the resort? When I had to tell him that my judgment was so bad that I'd married a man who cared only about what I or my family could do to make his life easier? That I was so stupid and naive I let my head be turned by flattery and empty promises?"

Maggie's amusement had faded during Hannah's bitter tirade. "Um, sis—"

"Or maybe I look better to him now," Hannah continued on a roll, gesturing meaningfully toward her midsection. "Accidentally pregnant at my age. Still paying off the bills my jailbird ex left me responsible for. Still so freaking angry and mortified that I—"

Hearing her own words, she stopped and shook her head. "Would you listen to me? Sorry, Mags, I guess the pregnancy hormones just kicked into overdrive. Seriously, I'm not interested in getting romantically involved with Andrew or anyone else. I tried the happily-ever-after thing and I failed miserably at it. Now all I need, all I want, is to make a home for my child, to ensure that he or she is loved and safe and happy while I continue with my work here. I really just don't have the time or the energy to take on anything else for the foreseeable future. So let's just drop it, okay? I'm turning in now."

Still looking concerned, her sister gave her a hug. "You'll call if you need me?"

"Of course, but I'm fine, really. Just tired. See you in the morning, okay?"

"Sleep in. We've got everything covered in the office."

"I'm ready to get back to work. Too much free time is obviously bad for my mood."

Only partially mollified, Maggie turned toward her own place, leaving Hannah to lock herself in her trailer, where she promptly covered her face with her hands and burst into tears, overwhelmed by the events of the day.

Andrew waited until both sisters were closed in their homes before turning and walking silently down the road. He stayed in the shadows, not wanting to be seen. He'd had enough experience with undercover work to be assured he was successful. His brother was preoccupied with Shelby, having moved into her trailer only that very afternoon, and the rest of the Bells were getting ready to turn in before starting another busy day early in the morning. Hoping to have a chance to talk privately with Hannah without anyone being the wiser, Andrew had told everyone good-night and said he wanted to take a walk before returning to his room for the night. That was how he'd ended up an unintentional eavesdropper on Hannah's conversation with her sister.

Making the half mile or so walk from the family compound to the motel, he took in the sights, sounds and smells of a summer evening in a camping-and-fishing resort. Only a few boats were still on the water at this hour. He heard the muffled roar of motors accompanied by glimpses of red, green and white running lights he spotted through the trees. Wisps of smoke from campfires drifted through the resort, and he fancied he could smell toasting marshmallows on the breeze. A few cars and pickups entered and exited the main gate, some towing boats after a day's water play. Muffled sounds were just audible from the campgrounds— bursts of laughter, the occasional high-pitched squeal from a child, a couple of yaps from what sounded like a small dog. An idyllic, slow-paced haven, it seemed far away from the hustle and bustle of the real world, a long way from Andrew's busy life in Dallas.

He paused at the intersection of the main road and the private drive, looking back over his shoulder at the dark stretch where Shelby had been taken. Proof, he thought grimly, of how easily the outside evils could invade even this diligently maintained paradise. While he was here, maybe he'd look over the resort's security practices. He wanted to make sure she—um, the whole family—was safe here, he quickly corrected himself.

That was the least he could do for Hannah for now. She'd made it clear enough that she wasn't interested in anything more from him.

It felt good to Hannah to be back at work after visiting her mother's family in Louisiana for the past ten days. She'd gone there to break the news to her extended family about her impending motherhood and had been gratified that her relatives on that side were as supportive as the Bell family. Her widowed grandmother was already busily crocheting a delicate baby blanket that she'd promised to mail as soon as it was completed.

She spent Tuesday morning taking reservations by phone, updating the resort's social media pages and website with new photos her sister had snapped around the place and checking in a few guests. Three thirty-something men with a three-day reservation for Cabin 5 wandered in just before noon, dressed in board shorts, T-shirts and sandals, ready for a few days of fishing and beer drinking. Judging by their behavior, Hannah suspected two of the three had gotten an early start on the latter; she hoped the other man had been the designated driver.

A tall, lanky man with a thinning mop of brown hair and beer-glazed brown eyes did an exaggerated double-take when he saw Hannah sitting behind the reception desk. He made a point of checking out her bare left hand, then smiled at her with what she assumed was meant to be irresistible charm. "Wow, when the owners of this place advertised beautiful scenery, they weren't kidding."

His two companions groaned in response to the outrageous pickup line. Well-accustomed to fending off passes from overly optimistic guests, Hannah merely smiled, looked at the reservation on her computer screen and asked, "Which of you is Nathan Burns?"

"That would be me," the supposedly sober man said. "Need my signature?"

She slid a form toward him. "Yes, please."

Skinny Romeo, as she'd mentally dubbed him, rested a hip on a corner of the desk. "The guys and I brought some big ol' steaks for the grill and plenty of beer and wine. Maybe after you get off work, you could join us for dinner?"

"Thank you," she said, barely glancing at him, "but I have plans. Linens and household items are provided in your cabin, but please let us know if you need anything. The convenience store, marina and grill in this building are open until seven."

"We brought Stu's fancy ski boat—it's a honey. Maybe you'd find a little time to go out on the water with us while we're here? We'll take a cooler full of beers on ice, have a great time."

"No," she said simply. "And please remember to have a designated driver when you're boating. BWI laws are strictly enforced on the lake. Let me get your keys for you."

She stood and opened the locked cabinet in which the keys to the cabins and motel rooms were stored. She heard a snort and a snicker behind her.

"Way to go, Bill. You've been hitting on a woman who's preggers," Stu said in a mocking whisper she probably wasn't supposed to hear.

"Not only that, he was shot down by her," Nathan added with relish.

Three keys dangling from her hand, Hannah turned to see Skinny Romeo—Bill—flushed with embarrassment, his eyes sparking with irritation. "You could have said something," he muttered to Hannah, who resisted pointing out that her condition was none of his business. And then he pasted on a forced, self-deprecating grin for the sake of his companions and shrugged. "Just practicing for all the bikini babes we'll be seeing on the beach the next three days."

Stu gave him a rough shove toward the door. "Like you've got a shot with any of them. Not to mention your fiancée would serve your innards to the dog if she found out. Now go on so we can get unpacked in time to do some fishing before dinner."

"Steffie's not my fiancée," Bill grumbled on the way out.

"Yeah, well, she sure seems to think she is," one of

the men retorted. Hannah didn't notice or care which because she'd already turned her attention to the next customer, an unaccompanied woman with faded red hair, heavy-lidded green eyes and frown lines carved around her unpainted mouth.

The woman was probably in her early thirties, pear-shaped, dressed in a too-tight T-shirt and denim capris with flip-flops. Her only attempt at makeup seemed to be the mascara that had smudged beneath her eyes. Hannah's instant impression was that of a woman who'd given up on her appearance for some reason. It was almost as if a gray cloud accompanied her into the building, a fanciful impression Hannah shook off impatiently.

"May I help you?" she asked with a welcoming smile.

"Jerks, huh?" the newcomer asked with a vague gesture toward the door through which the men had just departed. "I couldn't help overhearing some of what they were saying to you. You were pretty nice considering how pushy they were being."

Hannah didn't gossip about guests with other guests. "What can I do for you?" she asked without directly responding.

Accepting the hint, the woman nodded and tightened her grip on the red handbag she carried beneath one arm. "I'm looking for a motel room for a couple of nights. Someone in town told me this is a nice place to stay. I don't have a reservation."

"We have a few vacancies. Single or double?"

"Single. It's just me—I needed to get away from everything for a little while."

Hannah nodded and handed the woman a check-in form. "And how long will you be staying with us?"

"A few nights, I guess. Three, maybe four. Do I have to tell you now?"

Assuring the woman, whose name turned out to be Patricia Gibson, that she could stay as long as she wanted, Hannah completed the check-in and assigned her a lower-floor room in the motel. "We provide daily maid service unless you hang the do-not-disturb sign on your door. Linens, a mini-fridge and a flat-screen TV are also provided. Feel free to use the pool or lake swim beach, and there are grills and picnic tables in the day-use area by the beach."

She added the usual spiel for the diner and convenience store located on opposite sides of the reception desk. "Do you have any more questions?"

"It sounds real nice," Patricia murmured, picking up the key on a big plastic tag marked with her room number. "What was your name again?"

She had neglected to introduce herself, Hannah realized. She smiled apologetically. "I'm Hannah Bell."

The key clattered noisily on the tile floor when Patricia dropped it. Making a face, she laughed softly and bent to scoop it up. "That's why I needed a break. I'm so tired from working that my hands have gone clumsy. I'm sorry, I missed your name. Did you say Anna?"

"Hannah. Hannah Bell."

"Bell. So you own this resort?"

"It's a family business."

"I see." Tucking the key into an outside pocket of her purse, Patricia turned toward the door, but said over her shoulder, "This summer heat is a killer when you're pregnant, isn't it?"

"It can be," Hannah agreed lightly.

"I was pregnant this time last year. I had a miscarriage, though."

"Oh." Hannah struggled to think of something to say in response to the unexpected confidence. "I'm sorry."

Patricia shrugged. "It was for the best, I guess. I wasn't married. Hard to do it on your own."

Fortunately, she left before Hannah had to respond. It seemed to be her day for disconcerting encounters, a thought reinforced when Andrew wandered in.

He greeted her with one of his faint smiles that did not lighten his dark eyes, which were focused intensely on her face. "How's your day going?" he asked.

"It's been pretty weird so far," she replied candidly. "Yours?"

"I've been talking with your dad and your uncle about some new security measures for the resort. They've asked me to do a full analysis and make some suggestions."

Hannah nodded. "That sounds like a good plan. I hope you're charging them your standard consultation rates."

He merely gave her a look.

She sighed. "Andrew, you don't owe my family any favors. It's the other way around actually."

"We're not talking about money right now, though you and I need to make some arrangements soon."

She looked around quickly to make sure no one had overheard, but while she heard voices from the diner and the store, the reception area was deserted for now. "Andrew—"

"Well, hello, there." Mimi bustled up with a bright smile at finding Andrew talking with Hannah. "What are you two chatting about?"

Andrew turned easily to greet Hannah's grandmother. "I was just about to have lunch in the grill.
Thought I'd stop in to say hello to Hannah first."

"Hannah can join you for lunch," Mimi said, beaming. "I just came to relieve her at the desk for a while.
I've already eaten. I think I saw some of the other family in the diner, so you two run along and join them."

"I was going to have lunch a little later, Mimi," Hannah protested weakly.

"You need a break, sweetheart. No need to rush back,
I'll be fine here if you young folks want to take a walk
through the resort after lunch. There's a nice breeze
down by the water today."

So either her mom hadn't yet spoken to Mimi about
her matchmaking scheme for Hannah, or the talk hadn't
been successful. Hannah sighed, but knew there was
no use arguing with Mimi now, especially in front of
Andrew. She stood and smoothed the loose pink summer top she wore with thin khaki slacks. "Okay, fine.
I'll take my lunch break now."

Nodding in satisfaction, Mimi took her place behind the desk, pulling a thick paperback out of her bag
to occupy her until she was needed. Hannah knew her
grandmother would be quite content to spend the rest
of the day sitting in that comfortable chair with her
book, especially if she believed her granddaughter was
being courted by a respectable man in the meantime.
She didn't even want to think of the pressure Mimi—
and probably the rest of the family—would put on them
once they learned Andrew was her baby's father.

"Listen, maybe we could cut out of here and eat lunch
somewhere else?" Andrew asked in a low voice as soon

as they were out of her grandmother's sight and hearing. "We really need to—"

"Oh, hi, guys." Shelby slid in between them, looping her hands beneath their arms. "Heading in for lunch? So am I. I've been working on the books all morning without a break and now I'm starving. Aaron's supposed to meet me in the grill. Why don't you two join us?"

Andrew gave Hannah a look over her cousin's curly blond head, and she might have been amused under any other circumstances. It was rare to see Andrew looking totally flummoxed, but she thought that word was a good description for the expression in his narrowed eyes. He was probably beginning to wonder if they would ever have a chance to talk in private. She supposed she should be working harder to make arrangements for that discussion, rather than putting it off. But to be fair, he'd shown up only the day before. There hadn't been a lot of time for her to come to terms with all of this yet.

"Sure," Andrew said to Shelby, his tone completely bland. "We'd love to join you, wouldn't we, Hannah?"

She gave him a weak smile. "Why not?"

Andrew had not been this frustrated in a long time. He sat in his room Wednesday night at almost ten, uninterested in watching television. His computer screen displayed work-related data he should be looking over but wasn't. More than twenty-four hours after Shelby dragged Hannah and him into the diner for Hannah's lunch break, Andrew had yet to speak with Hannah alone again. Every time they'd been even close to a private conversation, one of her family members or a resort guest had interrupted them. Had he not been close to tearing his hair out with exasperation, the comedy of errors might have been wryly amusing. Or was Hannah deliberately using those seemingly random interruptions as an excuse to continue delaying their talk?

Too restless to stay put any longer, he let himself out of the room and headed out into the still-warm night air. He liked walking through the resort at this hour as campers and guests settled in for the night, making it possible to hear the crickets and frogs coming from the lakeside. He passed an older couple walking hand in hand along the road and swapped greetings with them. They, too, seemed to be enjoying the cooler temperature of evening. They looked comfortable together, he thought, glancing over his shoulder at them. Content to be spending their twilight years together.

Would he have anything like that when he reached their age?

He glanced toward the family compound and thought about slipping over to see if Hannah was awake. But, no. She needed her rest, and she wouldn't appreciate it if anyone in her family saw him making a late-night call on her. She was going to have to face telling her family the truth eventually—soon—but that wasn't the way she'd want to break the news to them.

He wished he understood better why she was so hesitant about revealing that he was the father of her child. He could understand that she'd be embarrassed about the awkwardness of the situation. But was there more to it than that? Was she worried about any claims he would make on their child? Had their one night together been so unsatisfactory for her that she'd bolted the next morning and was now sorry there was any reason for him to remain in her life? How was he to know if she wouldn't talk to him?

The glow of several campfires flickered through the trees from both the RV and tent campgrounds. A few cars passed, as did a couple on bicycles equipped with headlamps and reflector tape. As he strolled through the resort, Andrew made mental notes of areas that could use a little more security lighting—without over-lighting the campgrounds of course—and a few places where he would recommend installing discreet, closed-circuit cameras.

Outside Cabin 5, three men were rather loudly arguing outside on the porch. Andrew knew an alcohol-fueled conversation when he heard one. He hoped this one didn't get so rowdy that a sleepy guest in a neigh-boring cabin would feel the need to report it to man-agement, disturbing the Bell family. He knew the Bells were accustomed to those late calls, but he was sure they appreciated the uninterrupted nights.

"I'm telling you that girl on the beach was interested in me until you clowns ran her off by acting like fools. If I meet someone tomorrow, I want y'all to back off, you hear?" one of the men demanded loudly.

Another snorted mockingly. "Come on, Bill, she hardly looked twice at you. You think every woman you pass falls for you and most of the time you're wrong. Like with that pregnant girl in the office yesterday."

Andrew's steps slowed dramatically.

"Hey, you think she wasn't checking me out?" the first man asked. "If I was in the mood to tap a preggo, you can bet she'd be all over it. You didn't see a ring on her finger, did you?"

Andrew's fists clenched slowly at his side, even as the jerk's companions guffawed.

"Hell, Bill, you really are delusional. Pregnant or not, women who look like that don't go for guys like us. You better be content with Steffie and stop chasing the hotties or you're going to end up alone, dude."

"You don't know what you're talking about, Stu. Ever since Camille dumped you, you've been—"

"Hey!" Someone from Cabin 4 called out from his own front porch. "Could you guys keep it down? We've got kids trying to sleep in here. Don't make us call management."

"Yeah, okay, sorry." One of the men called back. "C'mon, guys, let's get some sleep. We're going out early to fish, remember? The three of us. Bros before... well, you know the rest."

The thought of that man—any man—hitting on Hannah made Andrew scowl as he stalked back to his room. His expression must have been forbidding. The frumpy redhead in the room below his jumped and gave a little gasp when he appeared out of the darkness. She must have just gotten back from a vending-machine run. She nearly dropped the canned soda in her hand when she saw him.

Trying to smooth his expression, he gave her a nod and kept walking. One way or another, he promised himself, he would be talking with Hannah tomorrow.

Chaos descended with a vengeance Thursday afternoon. A neighboring resort suffered a catastrophic septic-system malfunction, shutting the place down for the weekend at a minimum. Frantically dealing with disappointed vacationers, the owners referred as many as they could to the Bell Resort, sending the rest to other facilities along the lake. Every available RV pad and tent site at Bell Resort was filled, as were the cabins and motel rooms. Even the overflow area behind the boat storage was filled to capacity. The grill, convenience store and marina buzzed with activity. Every member of staff was almost running trying to keep up.

Leaving her cousin Lori to work the front desk, Hannah volunteered to run errands in town that afternoon. She visited the bank and the post office, dropped off some dry cleaning, then stopped by the locally owned pharmacy her family patronized to pick up prenatal vitamins for herself and prescriptions for several family members. She parked in a shady corner of the almost-empty little lot so her car wouldn't be quite so hot when she climbed back into it.

"Hello, Hannah. How are you today?" the pharmacist behind the counter asked with a welcoming smile after she'd been greeted by his two longtime employees. Short, round and mostly bald, his kind dark chocolate eyes gleaming in a polished ebony face, Luther Duquesne had served this community since Hannah was in grade school. He'd always had a lollipop for Hannah and Maggie when they'd come in with their mom, offered to them from a big glass jar filled with colorful treats. Even if he hadn't been one of the nicest men she knew, for that reason alone, Hannah would always have a soft spot in her heart for him.

Plugged in as he was to the community, he already knew about the disaster at the Lake Oaks Marina, so he and Hannah chatted about that for a few minutes while he checked her out. "Tell your grandpa this is his last refill on his blood pressure medicine. He needs to go see his doctor this month."

Hannah nodded. "I think he has an appointment, but I'll make sure."

"Before you go…" With a flourish, he presented her with an orange lollipop. "I seem to remember this being your favorite flavor."

She laughed and accepted the treat. "Thank you, Mr. D. I'm sure I'll see you again soon."

He winked at her. "I plan to be around to give a lollipop to that little one of yours. You take care, you hear?"

"I'll do that, thanks."

Carrying the bag of meds and her lollipop, she left the little pharmacy with a smile. That smile faded when she approached her car and saw the back left tire was flat. Her good mood vanished completely when she saw the front left tire, also flat. With a sinking heart, she walked to the other side of her car. Both tires on the right were pancaked. Visible punctures in all four tires provided an explanation, and the long ugly scratch in the paint from the front right fender to the back of the car called further attention to the vandalism.

Someone had intentionally done this.

Chapter Three

Stunned, Hannah turned in a slow circle, looking for a possible culprit, but it was time for the pharmacy to close for the day and hers was the only car left in the little lot. She saw no one else within view who might have done this. The shaded corner in which she'd parked wasn't particularly visible from the street. It wouldn't have been difficult for someone to walk past, swiftly slash her tires and scratch her paint and rush away without attracting attention. What she could not understand was why anyone would have wanted to do so. A random act of maliciousness? Wannabe tough-guy juvenile delinquents showing off for friends? Or—she swallowed hard—had her car been specifically targeted?

"Hannah," Luther called out from the door of the pharmacy, "are you all right?"

"Flat tires," she responded, trying to keep her tone

light. "Go ahead and close up your shop. I'll call some-one from the resort to come get me."

Frowning, he approached her, studying her tires with a shocked expression. "This is deliberate?"

"It seems to be."

"But who would do this?"

She wished she knew. With a shrug, she gave the only explanation that made any sort of sense to her. "Just some bored kid whose idea of fun is destroying other people's property, I guess."

Looking angry that this had happened at his store, Luther turned in a slow circle, much as Hannah had, looking for possible culprits. "Have you called the po-lice yet?"

"I hadn't even thought of calling the police," she admitted.

"Want me to call them for you?"

"No, I'll take care of it. I'm sure they'll have ques-tions for me."

He nodded. "I'm going inside to help the ladies close up, but I'm not leaving until someone has come for you. Why don't you come inside and get out of this heat? I'll get you something cold to drink while you wait."

"Thank you. I'll make some calls first and then come in."

"Let me know if you need anything."

"Thank you, Mr. D." Taking another look at the ugly scratch on the side of her car, Hannah swallowed hard before turning her attention to her phone.

Andrew took one look at Hannah's car in the phar-macy's small parking lot and ground out a curse. If his instincts were correct, this was more than just a random act of vandalism. And his instincts were almost always reliable.

Even though it was past the closing hour posted on the pharmacy door, he could see Hannah standing inside, looking out at him. She opened the door as he approached. "Hello, Andrew."

He studied her intently. Her expression was carefully shielded, but he saw the distress reflected in her deep green eyes. "Are you okay?"

"Yes, of course. I was inside when it happened. I never even saw anyone."

"Did you call the police?"

"I filed a report. Not that it will do any good, because there were no witnesses. And I've called for a tow truck. It should be here any minute."

He nodded. "We'll follow the tow truck and I'll wait with you at the body shop until your car is fixed. If they can't get to it today, I'll take you back to the resort and we can pick it up tomorrow."

Hannah nodded, then turned to speak to someone Andrew couldn't see inside the pharmacy. "A friend is here to give me a ride, Mr. D. Thanks for waiting with me."

"You take care," Andrew heard a man's voice reply. Hannah joined Andrew outside, and a friendly looking man locked the door behind her, nodding a greeting to Andrew through the glass before turning off the Open sign.

Hannah glanced up at Andrew. "I wasn't expecting you to be the one to come get me."

He shrugged. "Everyone else was busy with that influx of new guests, so I volunteered." He'd known he wouldn't have been her first choice, but no one else had seemed to find it unusual that he'd volunteered his services. He turned with Hannah toward her car. "You didn't see anyone who could have done this? No one walking or running away, even someone who seemed an unlikely culprit?"

"Several cars drove by, but I didn't see anyone at all on the sidewalk," she answered. "Trust me, I tried. Whoever it was either ran off before I came outside or hid while I was looking for them."

"You said you called the police. Did they mention whether there's been a rash of car vandalisms in this area recently?"

She shook her head. "Luther Duquesne—the pharmacist who waited with me—said this is the first he's heard of. He and the other pharmacy employees park in the back lot, but none of their vehicles were touched. Mine was the only one in this front lot, because it was almost closing time."

"Do you know anyone who would have specifically targeted your car?"

He noted the slightest hesitation before she shook her head. "I'm sure it was just a random act of meanness."

"Probably," he agreed. "But what name popped into your head just now when I asked?"

She lifted an eyebrow. "I beg your pardon?"

"You thought of someone. Who?"

Hannah sighed in resignation. "Okay, for just a second I wondered if it could have been—"

"Hannah," he urged impatiently when she hesitated again.

"My ex-father-in-law," she muttered, "Chuck Cavender. I ran into him and his wife earlier this week, and he still blames me for everything that happened to Wade."

"Wade is the only one to blame for everything that happened to him," Andrew said bluntly, angry at the thought of anyone placing responsibility on Hannah for her jerk of an ex-husband's behavior.

He knew for a fact that Hannah had done everything she could to hold her ill-fated marriage together. She'd been a hell of a lot better wife than Cavender had deserved, not that the bastard would ever admit it. For the most part, Andrew preferred not to think of Hannah with Wade—or anyone else, for that matter, he admitted privately and uncomfortably. "Do you have any reason to think Cavender might have done this? Did you see a vehicle that might have been his, either here or at one of your other stops this afternoon?"

She shook her head. "I really can't see him following me around or skulking in parking lots waiting for a chance to vandalize my car. He's more open with his disdain than that. It wouldn't surprise me if I ran into him and he made ugly accusations where other people could hear him, but doing something like this, in secret, without having the satisfaction of seeing my reaction? Doesn't seem likely."

A tow truck arrived while Andrew contemplated her rationale. The car was delivered to a shop, where Hannah was informed that it would be late the next day before she could pick it up again. Fortunately the scratch wasn't too deep and could be buffed out with rubbing compound rather than requiring repainting.

"I'll bring you back tomorrow," Andrew assured her when they were back in his car. "I'm sure everyone else is going to be snowed under with it being the start of a weekend and so many guests to juggle."

Fastening her seat belt with a snap, she said, "I have

a doctor's appointment tomorrow afternoon. I'll have to pick up the car after that."

"Then I'll take you to the doctor first." He was pleased to have the excuse to do so. "Didn't you say you're going to find out the baby's sex tomorrow?"

"Yes," she admitted, perhaps a bit reluctantly. "But—"

"I'd like to be there. Maybe we should tell your family about us tonight, before the doctor's appointment."

He could almost feel the waves of panic coming from her side of the car. "Um, not tonight," she said. "Everything's been so crazy at the resort today and everyone will be busy and tired."

He flipped the turn signal and turned the wheel, guiding the car into the empty parking lot of a bank branch that was closed for business for the day. Parked at the back of the lot, the car was partially hidden from the main road by the drive-through lanes. He left the motor running so the interior stayed cool as he unbuckled his seat belt and turned to face her. She wasn't looking at him, but down at the hands she held in a white-knuckled clench in her lap. She seemed braced for a lecture and something about her closed, defensive posture made his chest tighten.

Reaching out to lay his right hand over both of hers, he spoke quietly. "You should tell them when you're ready. They're your family. You'll know when the time is right."

He didn't find it particularly gratifying to see a hint of suspicion in the look she gave him, as if she were attempting to figure out if he was trying to manipulate her in some way. Once again he felt a wave of disgust at her duplicitous ex-husband for leaving her so wary and distrustful.

"Whatever you decide to do, I'll support you," he assured her. "Just let me know what you need from me."

He saw her throat work with a hard swallow, but he didn't give her a chance to speak before he continued, "It must have seemed to you that I swept back into your life and immediately started pushing you. That was not my intention. I have to admit I was rattled and I wasn't quite sure how to handle everything. Maybe I should have called before I just showed up, but most of the things we need to discuss seemed better handled face-to-face."

He thought he saw a softening in her eyes when she looked up at him then. "I'm sorry you had to find out the way you did," she said quietly. "I should have called you sooner."

He nodded. "Okay, we've got the apologies out of the way. We're both just playing this by ear."

"True."

"So?"

She drew a deep breath. "So, we take it from here. If you'd like to accompany me to the doctor tomorrow before we pick up my car, you're welcome to come, even though I'm sure Mimi will be much too pleased about it. For now, we'll tell everyone it's your way of helping out while everyone else is so busy this crazy weekend. Later, when things have settled down and after I have a doctor's report, we'll figure out a way to tell them you're my baby's father and then we'll deal with their reactions. When do you have to go back to Dallas?"

"I should be back in the office Monday," he admitted reluctantly, thinking of all the work that had piled up in his absence. He'd been trying to handle some of it from his hotel room the past couple days, but there were a few things he had to attend to in person. "I can come back next weekend, if that would be a better time for you. You, um, do want me to be there when you break the news, right?"

"Well, because I'm sure your brother is going to be around, you might as well be, too."

Her wry rationale wasn't exactly heartwarming, but he nodded. "Just let me know when you're ready," he repeated.

"Thank you," she said in little more than a whisper.

He realized he was still holding her hands, leaning quite close to her over the car's console between them. Her gaze was still locked with his, and he was momentarily trapped in liquid emerald. Despite all that had happened between them, all the uncertainty ahead, she still took his breath away. She was so beautiful, with her long-lashed eyes and full, sensuous mouth, her heart-shaped face framed in thick, dark, glossy hair. But it was more than her beauty that had always drawn him to her. He admired her courage, her dignity, the proud spirit her experiences had bruised but not extinguished.

She shifted in her seat, and he wondered if he was making her self-conscious.

"Are you uncomfortable?" he asked.

She smiled faintly. "The baby just kicked me in the side."

That, of course, drew his attention straight to her tummy. She was still so small that he hadn't really thought much about the baby's development. At almost six months along, it must be pretty well formed by this point, he realized. He wanted to feel the movement himself, but he knew better than to place a hand on her without permission. His female cousins who'd had children had often complained about people—even strangers—thinking they had a right to feel a pregnant woman's stomach.

Hannah seemed to read his thoughts. She took his hand and laid it on her swollen tummy, just above the seat belt she still wore. Only moments later, he felt a little thump beneath his palm. His eyes widened. "Was that it?"

"Yes. He's active this afternoon."

"He?"

She shrugged, her emotions well-masked, though her voice sounded a bit huskier than usual. "Just a figure of speech. This time tomorrow, I could be saying she."

He focused on his hand, his attention on the movement beneath it. He pictured a little girl who looked just like Hannah—or a boy with his own mother's big dark eyes. Both images made his chest tighten. He raised his gaze to look at Hannah only to find her studying his face with eyes that looked suspiciously moist. The next thing he knew, his mouth was on hers.

The console of Andrew's sports car dug into Hannah's left side. The baby kicked against her right rib cage. The still-fastened seat belt bit into her shoulder, and her left leg had twisted into an uncomfortable position. And yet she was in no rush at all to move out of Andrew's arms.

His mouth moved slowly on hers, his lips firm and gentle at the same time. The faintest hint of early evening shadow roughened his cheek when she laid her fingertips against it. His hand slid to the back of her head to hold her in place as he took his time exploring every inch of her willing mouth.

She had known the first time Andrew kissed her that there was a volatile chemistry between them, something she had suspected from the first time their eyes met. She'd tried to tell herself at the beginning that she was deluding herself, that she was confusing gratitude and attraction, that her stinging ego was pushing her to look for validation in a man's approval. But the more time she had spent with Andrew, the more she'd become aware of what a good man he was, and how much she genuinely admired and truly liked him. None of which had convinced her that they belonged together. Just the opposite, in fact. She had survived the end of her marriage with her heart battered but intact. Some instinct told her a bad outcome with Andrew would devastate her—not that he'd given her any reason to believe he was interested in pursuing a long-term relationship with her.

Slowly he drew back his head, leaving her lips damp, tingling, aching for more. Her throat clenched, her pulse raced, and her already-hormonal emotions threatening to overwhelm her. Her heart still ached from the look she had seen in his eyes when he'd felt their baby move. Between that and the kiss, she couldn't trust herself at all just then to think rationally.

She cleared her throat. Hard. And still her voice was hoarse when she said, "We'd better go. I called Mom from the body shop and told her we were on the way. They'll be wondering what happened to us."

She was relieved when he immediately drew back. Apparently he was going to stick to his promise that he was letting her set the pace now. At least until his patience ran out.

She heard him snap his seat belt back into place, but kept her face turned to look out the passenger side window. She needed to use the remainder of the drive to get her expressions under control before dealing with her family again.

"I moved out of my motel room while you were running your errands," Andrew said conversationally as he drove through the resort gate. "It seemed a waste for me to take up a room when every vacancy is in demand."

"That was generous of you." Hannah had no doubt that he'd had plenty of offers of spare beds from her family, since each household had at least one. "Where are you staying?"

"Steven's spare bedroom. The whole family volunteered, but I think I'd be most comfortable with Steven."

She bit her lower lip, realizing that Andrew would be staying right across a narrow road from her now rather than half a resort away in the motel. Great.

"Unless you'd rather I stay with you instead."

She whipped her head around in response to his comment. "What?"

Andrew slanted her a rare, playful grin that made him look even more like his lighthearted brother. "Just kidding."

Even though her lips twitched with an unexpected smile, she shook a finger at him. "Behave yourself."

His chuckle was more wry than amused. "If I'd done that, we wouldn't be in this situation, would we?"

Her cheeks warmed as erotic images flashed through her mind—again. "You hardly bear all the blame for that," she murmured.

He glanced at her and she thought she saw the shared memories heating his eyes. But rather than continuing the topic that had the potential to become awkward fast, he asked, "Where do you want me to drop you off?"

"At the main building. I have to bring some things to the office."

He nodded and took the right turn that led toward the lake.

It was after six now, but the resort bustled with activity. The day was still hot and bright, the lake still crisscrossed with fishing and ski boats and personal watercraft. The cordoned-off swimming area was crowded with families enjoying the cool water now that the sun had lowered a bit. Even when the resort was full with cool-weather campers, it always seemed oddly quiet in the winter months when the swimming area was closed. No lifeguard was provided at the swim-at-your-own-risk beach, but prominently posted signs reminded parents to closely watch their children. The shrieks and laughter drifting from that direction were familiar sounds to Hannah. The resort did good business year round, but summer, of course, was the prime source of annual income.

A gaggle of teenagers burst from the building as Hannah and Andrew approached, sodas and candy bars in their hands providing evidence that they'd visited the convenience store. A middle-aged couple who'd camped often at the resort for the past five years called out a greeting to Hannah as they made their way toward the boat slips with fishing rods in their hands. She waved back and wished them luck with their fishing outing.

"Did you ever get tired of living in the middle of a resort when you were growing up?" Andrew asked her as he reached around her to open the door. "Always being surrounded by so many people?"

"I'd have been surrounded by even more people if I'd grown up in an apartment in the city," she said with a shrug. "But at least here we had the lake and the playground and plenty of room to run and ride our bikes and skate. When I wanted time to myself, I could always retreat to my room or to a hammock in our backyard, because the family compound was off-limits to guests. Our parents taught us about staying alert around strangers, never running off alone, water safety and so on, but I'd say it was pretty much an ideal place to grow up."

"And you plan to stay here in your trailer after the baby's born?"

"That's the plan," she said lightly. "For a while anyway. At least I'll have plenty of family around to help out."

He looked as though he wanted to say something more, but now they were inside and surrounded by people, several of them relatives, so he couldn't.

"I'll see you later," she told him, already digging in her bag for the paperwork she had to drop off at the office and the prescription bottles to be delivered to various family members.

Andrew nodded and turned toward the diner. "Later," he said, making it sound like a promise.

Hannah saw her grandmother making a beeline in her direction, and she pointed a stern finger. "Don't even start," she warned. "You may ask about the errands I ran or what happened to my car, but no more matchmaking."

Mimi sighed dramatically, not even bothering to pretend ignorance. "Fine."

Nodding in satisfaction, Hannah handed her grandmother the prescriptions she had picked up for her, then headed for the office.

* * *

Between the pandemonium at the resort and Aaron's brand-new romance with Shelby, there had been little chance for Andrew and Aaron to speak privately since Andrew arrived. Andrew thought that was a good thing in some ways because it had always been so hard for him to hide anything from his brother. So he found himself on guard when he and Aaron were finally alone together at almost ten Thursday night.

They'd been playing a card game with Shelby and her parents and brother when a call had come in about some trouble at Campsite 32. C.J. had automatically risen to respond, but Aaron volunteered instead, reminding his girlfriend's father that he was the newest member of the employee roster and should be the one to take the night shift. Andrew had come along because it was time for the gathering to end and because he was curious.

They'd parted from Steven outside his parents' house. Because of his mending leg, Steven was getting around in one of the resort's green golf carts. Andrew had a key to Steven's trailer, where he'd be bunking for the night, and Steven urged him to feel free to let himself in and make himself at home when he returned from accompanying Aaron.

Andrew and Aaron hopped into another golf cart. It wasn't a long walk to the problem site but the cart would get them there more quickly. Aaron took the wheel. "I think I've memorized the grounds during the past week," he murmured. "If I'm right, site 32 is lakeside, almost in the center of the row."

"Sounds about right," Andrew agreed, calling on his own vague memory of the resort map. "What, exactly, is the problem we're responding to?"

"Noise complaint. C.J. told me it usually just takes a warning from management to get them to quiet down."

Andrew knew it was rare that local law enforcement had to be summoned to the resort, though it did happen occasionally. For general complaints, guests were encouraged to call the 24-hour service number, which was routed to various Bell family members, depending on who was on call for the night. For true emergencies, such as medical crises or other dangerous situations, they were instructed to call 9-1-1. Staying on the main road that circled through the resort, Aaron drove past two intersecting roads on the right, the first leading between rows of RV pads, the second through the tent-camping area. He swung right at the end of the road between another two rows of RV pads, the ones on the left located at the lakeside.

The pads were identified with reflective markers that glowed in the cart's headlamps, but they didn't need to read the numbers to know they had reached the right place. They could hear the raised voices even from several yards away. Swapping a look with Andrew, Aaron parked the cart in front of the double-cab pickup that had been used to tow the expensive fifth-wheel camper parked on the concrete pad. The windows of the camper had been cranked open to let in the cooler evening air, and the violent shouting inside was all too audible. A few crashes sounded along with the yells. Several people from nearby campsites hovered on the perimeters, looking toward the fifth-wheel in irritation, with curiosity and some concern. Aaron gave a wave to indicate that they should return to their own sites, and most of them did, with the exception of a few gawkers.

Andrew walked a step behind his brother as they approached the camper. Aaron still wore the green polo shirt with the resort logo, and he looked very official striding purposefully toward the camper. Andrew was still amused that this was the career that excited Aaron after the others he had tried had left him cold.

Aaron rapped on the door of the camper, firmly enough to be heard over the ruckus inside. A momentary lull was followed by the door being jerked open. Even standing to one side, Andrew could smell the reek of alcohol that wafted from the open doorway. An unsteady bear of a man with a sagging belly barely contained by a camo-print T-shirt over ragged denim cutoffs filled the doorway. "What?"

"Sir, I'm Aaron Walker. I work for the resort. We've had some complaints about the noise and I need to ask you to keep it down."

"Tell you what," the man snarled in response, "you tell those complainers that I'll mind my business and they can just mind their own."

Andrew swallowed a sigh. Didn't look like this would be an easy one.

He heard a woman's voice inside the camper. He couldn't make out all the words, but it sounded as though she were asking her companion, whom she called Neal, to calm down and come inside. The man looked over his shoulder and unleashed another string of curses, followed by a less-than-original threat for her to keep her mouth shut or else.

"I hope you won't make it necessary for me to call the authorities," Aaron told the jerk somewhat wearily. "It would be best if you go inside and sleep it off tonight so you can enjoy the rest of your stay with us."

Neal surged forward, his already-ruddy face going

even darker in the dim security lighting. "You know what I think would be best? I think it would be best if you just shut your trap."

Andrew moved forward to stand beside his brother, who shot him a warning look. Aaron was reminding him silently which one of them was the resort representative, and that he could handle this. Andrew merely shrugged, making it just as clear that he always had his brother's back.

Seeing a second man, Neal hesitated, frowning as he looked from Aaron to Andrew and back again. He blinked a few times, maybe wondering if the booze was affecting his vision, then snarled. "Seriously? They sent the Jonas brothers to give me orders?"

"Sir—" Aaron began, but didn't get a chance to finish the warning. The intoxicated Neal drew back a meaty fist and swung it toward Aaron's jaw. He never connected. Proving he still remembered the self-defense training he'd taken since he was a kid, Aaron blocked the wild punch, caught the man's arm, spun him around and had his face pressed against the side of the camper before the guy even knew what was happening.

There was no need for Andrew to help, but he shifted his weight meaningfully, prepared to do so if necessary. "Want me to call the cops?" he asked his brother, reaching for his phone.

Staring at Andrew with the eye not smashed against his camper, Neal sagged in surrender. "All right, let me go. No need to call the cops. There won't be any more trouble tonight."

"He's just tired," the chubby bleached blonde in the camper doorway said anxiously. "We got into an argument and it got out of hand. We'll be quieter now. Please don't call the police."

Aaron looked at Andrew as if to seek his opinion. Andrew paused a moment for effect, then nodded gravely. "I think you should give them another chance, Aaron. I doubt they'll disturb the other campers again tonight."

"We won't," the blonde promised breathlessly. "Will we, Neal?"

Straightening slowly when Aaron released him, Neal shook his head, looking resentful but cowed.

Bidding them both good-night, Aaron moved toward the golf cart, nodding toward the remaining onlookers, who returned to their own sites now that the confrontation had ended so anticlimactically. Andrew hopped into the passenger seat of the cart just as Aaron pushed the pedal to put it into motion.

"Might as well take a lap around the resort while we're out, just to make sure everything else is as it should be," Aaron commented.

Andrew nodded. "Sure. Why not?"

Aaron drove away from the camper in the opposite direction from the family compound. The campgrounds had fallen quiet now; 10:00 p.m. until 6:00 a.m. served as the official "quiet time" in the resort. As he had before, Andrew thought about how much he enjoyed the resort after dark. Strings of multicolored plastic lanterns in whimsical shapes decorated many of the campsites. Families and friends gathered around campfires, conversing in carefully modulated volume, only the occasional bark of laughter straying into noisier territory. Moonlight glittered on the inky lake waters spotted between the campers and trees. Overhead, stars were scattered across the cloudless sky. A battered old pickup truck with a rough-running motor passed them, then turned into the tent-camping zone, leaving a trail of smoky exhaust behind it.

He glanced at his brother, who was scanning the grounds as he drove. "Glad to see you remembered some of your training. Nice moves back there."

Aaron shrugged. "He was big, but more fat than muscle. And the booze didn't exactly enhance his speed or balance."

"Not to mention his judgment."

"That, too. I'm just glad he gave up as easily as he did. I'd have hated to get into a full-out brawl my first week on the job."

"You handled it well."

"Thanks, bro."

"No second thoughts about working here?"

"None. How could I get bored when there's something different to deal with every day?"

"You're basing your future career on your relationship with Shelby in some ways," Andrew felt obliged to point out. "It would be difficult for you to continue working here if you and Shelby split up."

"That's not going to happen."

Andrew twisted in his seat, genuinely curious. "How can you possibly predict that after only a couple of weeks with her? How do you know?"

Aaron's laugh was a bit sheepish but no less confident. "I just know. I've known almost from the minute I met her. It was like a bell went off in my head, you know? Like I heard this voice saying, 'Here she is, man. The one you've been looking for.'"

Gazing out the windshield of the cart, Andrew

thought of the other times he'd heard similar sentiments from members of his family, with their history of short courtships and long marriages. He'd always wondered if he would ever have that experience.

He remembered the first time he'd seen Hannah, the powerful impression she had made on him even then. He remembered the first time he'd kissed her, how every cell in his body had vibrated in reaction. He thought of the way she had stayed in his head since he'd met her, how her image had popped into his head at random and inconvenient times. He recalled every minute of the one night they had spent together, every touch, every sensation. Just as he remembered how hurt he'd been when she'd sent him away afterward, making it very clear that she saw that night as a one-time fling and that there was no need for him to contact her in the future. Neither of them had known, of course, that there would be a very compelling need for them to stay in touch for the foreseeable future as a result of that night.

Every time he saw her even now he responded dramatically. Was that love? Lust? Admiration? Shouldn't he know?

Sparks flew between them whenever they touched, but it was obvious that she was still wary of getting too closely involved with him. She'd told her sister that she didn't need or want a man in her life. Would she be fighting the attraction between them so fiercely if she were "the one"?

He knew now that his life and Hannah's would be intertwined for the next eighteen years, minimum. He had every intention of being involved in his child's life. As for the personal relationship between himself and Hannah—well, that remained to be seen. Unlike his brother, he had no confidence in his ability to predict his romantic future.

They said little as Aaron drove past the cabins, slowing a bit when he passed Cabin 7 where Shelby had been held at knifepoint, then speeding up to drive perfunctorily past the now-empty day-use area, the closed main building, the empty pool and quiet motel. A couple of teenagers were making out in the otherwise deserted playground, thrown into silhouette by security lights above them. Aaron drove on, leaving them to their youthful kisses.

Aaron parked the cart in the drive to the manufactured home he now shared with Shelby, next door to Steven's. Andrew glanced across the road, noting that lights still burned in both Maggie's and Hannah's trailers. Aaron followed his glance. "Anything you want to talk about, Andrew?"

Dragging his attention away from Hannah's bedroom window, Andrew asked, "Like what?"

"Like why you dropped everything and showed up here. You've been pretty evasive about that. At first I was sure you were here to talk me into going back home or to try to convince me to give myself more time to decide how I really feel about Shelby. Heck, I didn't even blame you. I can see how you and the rest of the family would be concerned about how fast this all happened. But that's not the only reason you came, is it? Something else seems to be bothering you."

Resisting an impulse to glance back at Hannah's place, Andrew shook his head. "I'm not ready to talk about it just yet."

Although he really wished he could. He wanted to talk with his brother about the shock he was still dealing with, the anxiety and uncertainty—even the eagerness—with which he contemplated his child's arrival. They would discuss all of those things after he and Hannah had broken the news. He could wait—but it wasn't easy.

Fortunately, Aaron chose not to press him just then. Which didn't mean he wouldn't eventually. Maybe Aaron was still too caught up in his own major life changes to pay much attention to Andrew's distraction, but more likely he was just biding his time until Andrew was ready to spill everything. Andrew was quite sure Aaron would become more insistent about answers as his twin's departure grew closer.

Andrew saw the curtains twitch at Hannah's bedroom window as he walked toward Steven's place after bidding good-night to his brother. Maybe she'd heard voices and had looked out to investigate. Was she watching him as he crossed the dimly lit yard? He had a brief urge to change direction and knock on her door, but he resisted. He would see her tomorrow when he accompanied her to the obstetrician. He anticipated that visit with a mixture of nerves and eagerness. He wondered how Hannah was feeling just then.

He looked over his shoulder just in time to see the curtain fall back into place. Pausing with key in hand at the door of Steven's trailer, he smiled, though he doubted she was still watching. "We'll talk tomorrow, Hannah," he said aloud, and even though she couldn't hear him, the words were a promise.

Chapter Four

Friday dawned cloudy with a chance of rain later that afternoon. The gray-mottled skies didn't notably discourage the summer-morning lake enthusiasts; if anything, the slightly cooler temperatures had brought out even more early boaters, fishermen and swimmers. Fridays were always busy in summer, kicking off three-day breaks for many guests, but this weekend would be especially hectic with the additional business from the unlucky neighboring resort. Hannah and her family had been forced to scramble to work in the extras along with the standing reservations for the next few days.

Hannah enjoyed a slight breeze on her face as she walked to the main building at a quarter till nine, after breakfast at her place. Golf carts and utility ATVs were readily available to the family for getting around the resort quickly, and bicycles were parked beside all the family homes, but Hannah preferred to walk most of the time. She figured that would be more difficult as already-hot June became blazing July and she became more heavily pregnant. She decided she'd better enjoy a cool morning while she could.

She exchanged smiles, nods and greetings with guests and employees she passed en route. As she drew closer to the main building, a shriek from the swimming pool on her right drew her attention and she smiled when she saw that it was already filled with kids being supervised by coffee-sipping parents. It was a good way to burn off the children's morning energy, and too early to have to worry about sunburn.

"Good morning."

Hannah glanced at the woman who'd murmured the greeting from just behind her and smiled in recognition. She searched her memory for a name, hoping she had it right when she said, "Good morning, Ms. Gibson. Are you enjoying your stay with us?"

The other woman reached up to push a limp strand of faded red hair from her red-splotched face. The hollows beneath her eyes hinted at sleepless nights and she didn't even try to return Hannah's smile, though she spoke politely enough. "You can call me Patricia. And yeah, it's nice here. I was just going to pick up a pack of doughnuts or something from the store for breakfast."

"We serve an excellent breakfast in the grill," Hannah suggested, thinking that this seemed to be a very unhappy woman. "Three dollars will get you a cup of coffee or juice and an egg-ham-and-cheese sandwich on an English muffin. Or there are always fresh-made muffins. My aunt usually bakes blackberry muffins on Fridays. They're excellent."

Patricia looked less than enthusiastic about the recommendations. "I'll probably just eat in my room. Maybe on the balcony. Got a book I've been reading. It's not all that good, but I might as well finish it now that I've started it."

Goodness, this woman was a downer, Hannah couldn't help thinking. Either she was just naturally the morose type, or the personal trials she'd mentioned when checking in had left her depressed and weary. Because there was no way to find that out without prying, Hannah settled for making her smile extra warm as she held the door open for the guest. "Let us know if you need anything at all."

Patricia nodded. "I will. Thanks."

People milled inside the entryway, entering and exiting the store and grill or standing around the reception desk. Mimi had opened the desk at seven, a long-standing tradition she maintained by choice. Hannah always relieved her at nine—as Lori had while Hannah was away for the past couple of weeks. At a spry, still-sharp seventy-nine, Mimi was far from ready for full retirement, though her eighty-year-old husband had relegated most of his former duties to his sons. Pop preferred to take it easy now, hanging out around the marina, pitching in when needed, but mostly just shooting the breeze with guests, many of whom he'd known for years.

Carrying a clipboard and a travel cup of coffee, Maggie came down the stairs from the private offices above. Seeing Hannah, she smiled. "Good morning. Sleep well?"

"I did, thank you," Hannah lied blithely. "Maggie, this is Patricia Gibson, a guest in our motel. Patricia, my sister Maggie Bell. She's in charge of maid service, so be sure and let her know if you have any problems or requests."

"It's nice to meet you, Ms. Gibson," Maggie said with her usual warm smile. "I hope everything is satisfactory in your room?"

"Oh, yeah, it's a real nice place," Patricia replied, her tone devoid of emotion. "No complaints."

Maggie nodded. "Let us know if that changes."

"Good morning, ladies."

Just the sound of Andrew's voice made Hannah's heart take an extra-hard thump. She hoped she hid that reaction when she turned to greet him as he and Steven came out of the diner, her cousin more confident now on his crutches. "Good morning," she and Maggie said in chorus, while Patricia murmured something inaudible.

Nodding to them all, Andrew kept his eyes on Hannah. "Steven and I are going out to fish for a couple of hours, but I'll be available to drive you to the doctor's appointment and to pick up your car because everyone else is crazy busy today. What time do we need to leave?"

He had spoken breezily, as if it were no big deal at all that he would be the one giving her a lift, and Hannah hoped the others accepted it that way. "My appointment is at two-thirty, so I'll need to leave just before two. But if there are things you'd rather do on your vacation, I'm sure one of the others—"

Andrew was shaking his head before she could even finish the sentence, just a hint of reproach in his dark eyes. "There's no need to take anyone else away from their work when I have the whole afternoon free. I'll meet you here at one-fifty."

She nodded in surrender, trying to ignore her sister, who was watching a bit too closely. "Thank you."

He gave her a little salute as he and Steven headed for the marina. "See you."

Looking more glum than ever, Patricia headed toward the store. "Y'all have a good day," she mumbled over her shoulder to Hannah and Maggie.

"I've seen her around the motel the past couple of days," Maggie whispered to Hannah when the other woman was out of hearing distance. "Don't think I've seen her smile once. I wouldn't say she's having a great time, but she hasn't caused any problems or lodged any complaints."

"I feel sort of sorry for her," Hannah murmured in reply. "She seems very unhappy."

Three men shoved noisily out of the diner, almost colliding with the sisters. Hannah repressed a wince when she recognized the man she still thought of as Skinny Romeo. His narrow face flushed when he saw her, and one of his companions elbowed him meaningfully. Apparently his friends were still giving him a hard time because he had hit on a pregnant woman, which she found vaguely insulting even though she hadn't welcomed his advances. Nodding, the men headed for the exit while Hannah walked to the desk to relieve her grandmother, who'd been occupied on the phone ever since Hannah had entered the building. Maggie followed.

Hanging up, Mimi stood when Hannah rounded the desk. "We're still getting tons of calls asking for reservations for the July 4th week," she said with a shake of her silver head. "Some folks don't take it too well when I tell them we're full for the holiday."

"Then they should have booked earlier," Hannah said with a shrug, stashing her small shoulder bag in a drawer behind the desk. "Anything else I need to know?"

"That about covers it. So I understand Andrew will be your personal chauffeur this afternoon?"

Hannah shot her grandmother a look of warning. In response, Mimi chuckled and held up her hands. "I was just going to say how nice it is of him to step in when everyone else is so busy today. Those Walker boys are good men. You can tell they were raised right."

Even though she didn't believe for a minute that Mimi wasn't still matchmaking, Hannah nodded. "I appreciate all the help both of them have given our family," she said noncommittally.

Mimi had the tact to let it go then. "I'll go see if I can help your mother in the store. She's already had a steady stream of customers this morning."

Knowing how busy everyone was, Hannah was a little surprised her sister was still hanging around the desk. Taking advantage of a quiet moment with just the two of them, Maggie leaned a hip against the desk and tossed back her sun-streaked brown hair. "Did you notice the earrings I'm wearing today?"

Hannah recognized the casual set. Three silver chains in graduated lengths dangled from each earring. The chains ended in little metal balls, one gold, one silver, one copper. "I gave them to you for Christmas."

Maggie nodded, making the chains dance with the movement. "I love them. Wear them all the time. You picked them up in Dallas, didn't you?"

The too-casual question made Hannah's muscles tighten. "Um, yes. Why?"

"Just a comment. You know, it occurs to me that I never asked and you've never commented—did you happen to run into Andrew while you were in Dallas that weekend?" While the question was asked lightly, the expression in Maggie's eyes was quite serious.

Hannah should have known her sister would be the first in her family to put the clues together. She didn't know if Aaron had figured it out yet—or if Andrew had told him, though she didn't think he had—but then Aaron wasn't necessarily aware that she'd been in Dallas in December. She cleared her throat, trying to decide what to say.

The buzz of the phone was a welcome distraction. She reached for it quickly, giving her sister an apologetic shrug.

"We'll talk later," Maggie mouthed.

Hannah nodded, handling the reservations call by rote while watching her sister leave the building. The discussion with her family loomed ever closer. Perhaps Andrew was right that it would be best to get it over with soon.

He would be leaving Sunday. Everyone planned to meet at her parents' house tomorrow evening for one last big gathering before Andrew left. Maybe that would be the best time for the announcement. She felt her throat tighten just at the thought of the pandemonium that would surely follow, but it had to be done. As happy as she was about becoming a mother, she couldn't help wishing the circumstances were different. That was only normal, she assured herself, patting her tummy apologetically.

She stayed busy for the next few hours, which was a good thing because it didn't allow her too much time to fret. She wasn't really hungry at lunchtime, so she sipped a strawberry-banana smoothie at the desk, washing it down with water from the bottle she'd kept filled all morning in preparation for her ultrasound.

Lori showed up a few minutes early to fill in while Hannah was at the doctor's office. She wore her usual floaty garments in her typical gray color palette, though she'd added a touch of lavender this time with a very pretty sheer scarf. Despite her somewhat limited choice of color, Lori definitely had a knack for wearing her wardrobe like a supermodel.

"You look nice," Hannah told her.

Lori smiled faintly. "Thanks. I have a date later."

"Oh."

Lori frowned. "Now, don't you start. I get enough of the disapproving looks from everyone else in the family."

"I didn't say anything," Hannah reminded her.

"I got the message anyway." Her cousin scowled as she tossed her gray leather bag beneath the desk. "None of you know Zach, but all of you disapprove of him. It's not fair."

"How can we know him when you haven't even brought him around to meet us?" Hannah asked reasonably. "No one even knew you were dating him until last week."

"Yeah, right. Like I'm going to bring him here to be grilled by everyone in the family. God knows what Mimi or Pop would say to him."

Hannah shrugged. "That's true, of course, but it's just the way it is here. Maybe if the family got to know Zach they'd be less disapproving."

"Or maybe they'd still hate him," Lori muttered.

"That's possible, too, I guess. And if they do, well, maybe you should consider the reasons why."

Lori planted her hands on her hips. "You're saying I should let the family decide who I can or can't date?"

Hannah sighed. She was making a mess of this, probably butting in where it was none of her business. But still she felt compelled to offer advice in hopes that she could help Lori avoid the mistakes she herself had made. "I didn't say that. It's just— Well, you know what kind of mess I got into when I married too young and somewhat impulsively. I'd hate to see you get into that sort of situation."

"Yes, well, I'm not you. And Zach's not Wade. And thanks for giving me credit for having some intelligence."

Hannah frowned. "I like to consider myself reasonably intelligent. I still made a mistake by marrying Wade."

"So now you're going to give me advice?" Lori looked pointedly at Hannah's baby bump. "Thanks, but no, thanks."

"Hey!"

"Good afternoon, ladies."

Hannah wasn't surprised that Andrew had showed up exactly when he'd said, at precisely one-fifty. He'd changed from the shorts and T-shirt he'd worn for fishing into a white short-sleeved shirt and khaki pants. She didn't know how he'd managed to keep his hastily packed clothes so crisp and tidy or look so put together and professional even after a morning in a fishing boat. Whatever magic he used, it worked for him. He looked great, making her glad she'd taken a little extra care with her own appearance that morning. She wore a loose plum-colored top and cream linen drawstring slacks—summery, comfortable and easy to move out of the way for the ultrasound.

She turned the desk over to her now-rather-sullen cousin, trying and failing to meet Lori's eyes. Maybe she should have kept her mouth shut, she thought regretfully. She supposed nobody could have talked her out of getting involved with Wade either, but she sure wished someone had tried.

She stopped in the store to speak with her mother on the way out. Her dark hair hardly touched with gray, fifty-three-year-old Linda Bell handled the register in the bustling convenience store with an ease Hannah had always admired. Her mom might have married into the resort business, having grown up the daughter of a physician and a school principal, but she'd taken to it with the same enthusiasm as the rest of the extended family, making the store her own realm while her husband ruled over the grounds outside.

Leaving her mother-in-law to run the register for a few minutes, Linda walked to the end of the sales counter to give Hannah a hug. "You're leaving for the doctor now?"

Hannah nodded. "I'll let you know as soon as I'm back." She knew her family would be anxious to hear the results of the test.

Her mom looked a bit wistful. "You're sure you don't need me to come with you? I'm sure Mimi could handle things here for a little while," she added though she didn't sound entirely confident as she glanced at the customers filling plastic handbaskets with supplies from the shelves.

"I'll be fine. The appointment won't even take very

long," Hannah assured her. "Afterward, I'll pick up my car and come straight back to the resort. You're needed much more here."

Her mom nodded to concede the point. "Still, I'm glad you aren't going alone. I'm sure that tire-slashing incident was just random yesterday, but it still made me nervous."

Hannah shook her head indulgently. "I'm not going to stop running errands just because some punk flattened my tires. If my car hadn't been ready to pick up this afternoon, I'd have just borrowed someone else's and driven myself to the doctor."

"Yes, I know you would," her mom said wryly. "But I'm glad Andrew is going with you today. Thank you for volunteering, Andrew. Someone else would have taken her if you weren't here, of course, but I have to admit it's a big help to us that you're available."

Andrew drew his attention away from a couple of young boys nearby to smile at Hannah's mother. "It's my pleasure. I've never been very good at doing nothing. I prefer making myself useful."

Before she could reply, Andrew moved to block the doorway as the two boys tried to exit. "Maybe you'd better pay for that candy before you leave," he suggested to them, nodding toward the pockets of their colorful board shorts.

One of the boys started to bluster a denial, but a look from Andrew had him falling sullenly silent.

"Empty your pockets," Andrew suggested while Hannah's mother joined them, hands on her hips in a sternly maternal posture.

Red-faced, the boys turned over the candy they'd tried to smuggle out. Hannah knew they'd never have gotten even that far had her eagle-eyed mother not been distracted; fortunately, Andrew had been alert. No surprise.

"Dustin, your parents have been camping here since before you were born," Linda scolded as she set the candy on the counter. "Having a friend with you this weekend does not give you permission to break the rules of the resort."

Teary-eyed, young Dustin gave his scowling friend—the one who'd been most resistant—a look that made Hannah suspect who'd been the instigator of the would-be crime. "You aren't going to tell my parents, are you, Mrs. Bell? I won't do it again, I promise."

"I should tell them," Linda answered sternly. "I've know them long enough to be certain that they would want to know about this. This isn't the way you've been raised, young man."

A tear trickled down one freckled, sun-burned cheek. "No, ma'am. I'm sorry," he muttered.

Andrew narrowed his eyes at the other boy, who still looked a bit too defiant. "I haven't heard an apology from you."

The boy lifted his chin, mouth stubbornly closed.

Dustin elbowed his companion sharply. "Tell them you're sorry, Quentin. Geez, you don't want them to tell my dad."

"Sorry," Quentin mumbled, his voice barely audible, his eyes half-hidden beneath his mop of sandy hair.

"Run along now," Linda told them. "I'll have to think about this. I expect you to behave during the remainder of your visit with us."

The boys surged toward the door. Andrew took his time moving out of their way.

"You're really going to let them get away with that without telling their parents?" Hannah asked her mom, a bit surprised.

"Never said *I* wouldn't tell them," Mimi piped up from behind the register, frowning with disapproval.

Hannah's mom shook her head. "I'll handle it. I'll make sure Kelly knows that they need to keep an eye on their son's new friend."

She looked then at the other customers, several of whom had been watching with various degrees of subtlety. A small group of teenagers in the back of the store were nervously eyeing Andrew, keeping the sodas they'd taken out of the cooler in clear view to make sure he knew they weren't planning to steal them. "Can I help anyone?" Linda offered cheerily, causing the teens to rush toward the front with their drinks.

Waving goodbye to her mother and grandmother, Hannah rushed Andrew out of the store. They still had plenty of time to get to the doctor's office, but she preferred being early to taking the risk of running late.

"Those kids were kind of young to be running around the resort unsupervised, weren't they?" Andrew commented once they were on the road, Hannah giving directions from the passenger seat of his car.

"Dustin's ten or eleven, I think, and I assume his friend is the same age. We do prefer preteens to be supervised on the resort, but I guess his parents thought it was safe to let them come to the store for candy— though I'm sure they were expected to pay for their treats."

"For security and safety purposes, maybe you should make an official rule about unsupervised kids in the park."

She smiled. "Always on the job, aren't you, Andrew? Through the years, we've had problems with especially wild or unsupervised kids, but it usually only takes a few words with the parents from Dad or Uncle C.J. to settle the issue. On the rare occasions when situations got out of hand and the parents caused as much trouble as the kids, they were asked to leave—occasionally with an official escort from local authorities. We hate to resort to that—no pun intended—but when it's necessary, we do."

"My parents would have wanted to know if Aaron or I were ever caught trying to steal something from a store," Andrew commented. "We might have broken a few rules in our time, but neither of us ever tested that particular one. Mom would have dragged us by the ears to apologize to the owners, and Dad would have made very sure we never even thought of pulling that stunt again. He never laid a hand on us in anger, but he had his ways of getting his point across—mostly involving chores, bedtimes and video game privileges."

Hannah thought of her grandmother's comment that she could tell the twins had been raised right. "Whatever they did, it worked out well."

He shot her a smile. "Why, thank you. I believe that was a compliment."

She laughed softly. "It was."

His smile faded. "I've always hoped if the time came, I'd be as great a dad as my own. That my kid would feel about me the way I do about him."

She bit her lower lip. He'd probably also hoped he'd be able to raise his child full-time, rather than on custody visits she assumed would be their eventual arrangement. As much as she hated the thought of all those future goodbyes, she wanted her child to know a father's love and guidance, just as she had been fortunate enough to have all her life. She had no doubt that Andrew would be a wonderful father. He seemed to excel in everything he did, which she had to admit was more than a little daunting to someone who'd made so many mistakes in her own life.

She looked out the passenger side window as Andrew stopped at a red light. She groaned when she saw the man in the pickup beside them glaring back at her.

"Problem?" Andrew asked.

"Ex-father-in-law." Of course she'd seen Chuck today. It just seemed inevitable, for some reason.

Andrew looked at the truck with narrowed eyes. "Interesting that he just happens to be at the same intersection today."

Hannah shrugged. It was not so unusual really that she occasionally ran into Chuck, considering he lived less than ten miles from the resort, but she figured it was going to be awkward every time, no matter how many years passed.

The light changed and Chuck peeled away with a squeal of rubber on pavement.

Andrew accelerated at a more reasonable pace. "I think I need to look a bit more closely at Chuck Cavender," he murmured. "I don't like that he showed up today right after your tires were flattened yesterday."

She was still reluctant to consider the possibility that her former father-in-law had taken such petty revenge against her. "Chuck's not stalking me, Andrew," she said, hoping very much that she was right. "He lives nearby. It's just coincidence that we were at the same intersection at the same time."

"Yeah, well, he'd better stay far away from you in the future." The words were as close to a threat as she'd ever heard usually easygoing Andrew utter.

At the office of her obstetrician, Dr. Lena Power, Hannah checked in at the desk and was instructed to have a seat in the waiting area. Except for one other very pregnant woman accompanied by a man and a sleepy toddler, the tidy peach-and-green-decorated waiting room was empty and quiet. Tuned into a home decorating network, a television set played in one corner of the room. Stacks of parenting magazines were spread on tables near the seats. Andrew flipped through the pages of one that looked fairly recent, though he didn't stop to read any articles.

Hannah shifted nervously in her seat. She had suggested to Andrew that he could drop her off and entertain himself elsewhere until she called him to pick her up, but he'd said only that he had nothing better to do. He'd be fine in the waiting room, he'd assured her. He had a couple of books he'd been meaning to read stored on his phone.

"Hannah Bell?"

She looked up to see Dr. Power's nurse, Dana, standing in the doorway that led back to the exam rooms. Rising, she nodded. "I'm here."

Dressed in bright purple scrubs, Dana smiled and backed against the door to hold it open, Hannah's file tucked into the crook of one of her arms. "Come on back, we're ready for you. Is this the dad?" she asked, nodding brightly toward Andrew.

Hannah cleared her throat. "Um, yes," she said without meeting Andrew's eyes. She might as well get used to saying it. It wasn't as if Dana or the doctor would be seeing her family before she broke the news to them.

"You're both welcome to come back, if you'd like."

Hannah glanced automatically at Andrew then. He sat without moving, giving her the option, but she knew what he wanted her to say. "Would you like to see the ultrasound?"

He was on his feet almost before she finished the question, his dark eyes searching her face. "If you don't mind."

She didn't know quite how she felt about it actually, but this wasn't the time to analyze her emotions. She knew only that she wouldn't have felt right denying him this opportunity. She gestured to him to follow her as she turned to enter the exam area.

Ten minutes later, she lay on her back on the narrow, paper-covered exam table, her blouse raised to just below her breasts, the waistband of her pants lowered to below her navel, exposing her midsection. Andrew sat in a chair on her left side, while the sonographer, a stocky redhead who'd introduced herself as Melinda, stood at the right side of the table with the ultrasound wand in hand. After squirting a slimy—and cold—gel on Hannah's tummy, Melinda pressed the wand against her skin. All eyes were fixed on the monitor above Hannah's feet.

Andrew surged to his feet to lean closer when the gray-scale images began to appear on the monitor. He made a low, strangled sound in response to his first sight of his baby's face. Eyes, nose, mouth, ears. Hannah blinked rapidly against a surge of tears as she mentally cataloged all the features.

"Look at the little hands," she whispered to Andrew,

watching the tiny fingers open and close, almost as if waving hello.

Andrew's hand closed over hers, their fingers intertwining. He seemed to be at a loss for words, a sentiment Hannah could certainly understand. After all, she'd had longer than he had to get used to this idea, had even seen an ultrasound before, though the baby had been just a little peanut with nubs for limbs then.

The wand continued to scan, displaying the umbilical cord, little legs pedaling lazily, miniscule nubbins of toes. Positioning the wand just so, Melinda smiled warmly. "She's being very cooperative. Almost as if she's posing for us."

Andrew's fingers tightened spasmodically around Hannah's. "She?" he repeated huskily.

"She." Melinda pointed to the screen, showing them the proof. "It's a girl."

Andrew sat down abruptly in his chair, as if his knees had given out on him. Because he was still holding her left hand, Hannah swiped at her eyes with her right, her gaze locked on the monitor. Her daughter. *Their* daughter, she corrected herself with a hard swallow, glancing sideways at Andrew.

He looked a little pale. He tugged at the collar of his shirt with his right hand, as if it felt a little tight despite the top two buttons being unfastened. And then he drew his gaze from the screen, met her eyes and smiled. "She's beautiful."

She felt one tear escape to trickle down her left cheek. "Yes, she is."

Still clasping her hand, he leaned over to brush his lips over hers. And Hannah could almost feel the crack widen in the emotional wall she'd tried so hard to maintain between them.

Each clutching a still photo of their daughter, Hannah and Andrew met briefly with the obstetrician afterward. Hannah made the introductions. "Dr. Power, this is Andrew Walker. The, um, the father."

If she noted the hesitation before the acknowledgment, the tall, slender physician didn't let it show in the warm smile that lit her face. Hannah had always thought her fortyish doctor had the world's greatest cheekbones, high and pronounced in a tanned face framed by straight dark hair that strongly suggested a Native American heritage. "It's nice to meet you, Mr. Walker."

Andrew shook her hand with his usual easy charm.

The doctor visited with them for a few minutes, said that everything looked good so far for a mid-September arrival, and asked if either of them had any questions. Hannah glanced at Andrew, who shook his head.

Afterward, Hannah checked out at the desk and scheduled her next appointment in four weeks—after which she would see the doctor every two weeks as the delivery date drew closer. She wondered if Andrew would be with her at the next appointment. She could tell he made a mental note of the date and time.

She glanced at her watch as they left the doctor's office. "We'll have to go straight to the shop to pick up my car before they close."

Her car was obviously the last thing on Andrew's mind, but she welcomed the errand. The past half hour had been so emotionally draining that she needed to focus on something as mundane as new tires and buffing compound. Fortunately, the tire and body shop was only a couple miles from the doctor's office, so there was no time to talk on the way. She could see the frustration on Andrew's face when he tried once or twice to discuss their situation and she responded only with directions to the shop.

"Maybe we could stop somewhere for coffee before we go back to the resort? Or maybe a cup of green tea would be better for you?" he suggested as he turned into the shop parking lot.

"I'd better head straight back," she said, twisting the strap of her bag around her fingers. "Everyone is waiting to hear the baby's sex."

He started to say something, then fell abruptly silent. She suspected he had remembered his promise that they would talk only when she was ready. He probably wished now that he hadn't made that promise.

Taking pity on him, she sighed. "I know you think I've been procrastinating with you, and you're right. I have. But it's time for me to face the music. Why don't you come by my place tonight and we'll have a long talk. I know it's past due."

Rather than looking gratified, Andrew frowned. "You don't have to make it sound like you're scheduling a root canal."

She winced. Had she really sounded so unenthusiastic? "Sorry."

He nodded in resignation. "I suppose you want me to slip over without anyone noticing?"

Because that was exactly what she wanted, she merely shrugged lightly.

Andrew nodded again. "Let's get your car. I'll follow you back to the resort."

She could have gotten back just fine on her own, of

course, but she knew she'd be wasting her time to suggest he just drop her off and head back.

She took a deep breath before reaching for the door handle. Even though it was late in the afternoon, she still had much to do before she could sleep that night. Not the least of which was that stressful, but inevitable, discussion with her daughter's father.

Even though the promised rain had not yet developed by the time they returned to the resort, the clouds had continued to gather all day so that the sky was gray and low. An occasional rumble of thunder sounded in the far distance, warning of the rain on its way. The lake was beginning to empty, a bit earlier than usual at this time of year, in anticipation of potential lightning strikes. Andrew passed several vehicles pulling boat trailers leaving the resort as he drove through the gates behind Hannah. Still, the resort was so busy there wasn't even an extra parking space in front of the main building. Andrew assumed business was always brisk on a summer Friday afternoon, even when bad weather threatened, but he knew the extra guests from the closed resort added to the crowds. He drove around to Steven's mobile home to park in the drive there, seeing that Hannah had parked in front of her own.

He climbed out of his car to be greeted by Steven's big yellow dog. Andrew rubbed the lab's ears. "Hey, Pax. How's it going?"

The dog wagged its tail, and leaned companionably against Andrew's leg. Andrew chuckled wryly, thinking that this was probably the worst guard dog on the planet. He was much too lazy to chase off any trespassers.

"Mom just rang me," Hannah called from across the

road. "Most of the family is hanging around the grill waiting to hear from me."

Giving the dog one last pat, he then crossed over to join her. "Did you tell your mom yet that the baby is a girl?"

She shook her head with a wry smile. "She wanted to wait and hear at the same time as everyone else. Perhaps you've noticed that my family likes to turn everything into an event."

"As a matter of fact, I have noticed that."

She pushed a hand through her dark hair, brushing it off her face. Thunder sounded again, a bit closer this time, drawing her eyes to the darkening sky. "I was going to walk over, but maybe I'll take a cart instead. Looks like those clouds could open up any minute."

He noted the faintest of purple shadows beneath her eyes. "You've had a long day," he said, reaching out to stroke back a strand she'd missed. He let his hand linger on her cheek. She felt warm. Soft. Silky.

Their eyes locked and held. His thumb moved against her cheek, savoring the feel of her. His mouth was close to hers, and it would take only a slight movement on his part to have their lips pressed together. She moistened her lips with the tip of her tongue, and he knew she was thinking along the same lines.

Whatever other problems they faced, the attraction between them had never been in doubt. All it took was a touch or a shared look to set it off again. He couldn't imagine that ever changing, at least not on his part. Even tired, a little disheveled, worried and pregnant, Hannah looked beautiful to him. He wanted her. And he suspected she knew it.

He dropped his hand, knowing this wasn't the time. "Golf cart?"

She blinked. "Um, what?"

There was some satisfaction in knowing that brief interlude had left her mind a little hazy, especially because it had taken some effort to clear his own. "You were going to take a cart to the diner? I'd be happy to chauffeur you."

"Oh. Right." Her cheeks a little flushed, she stepped away from him. "Sure, if you're going that way anyway."

"Are you kidding?" He chuckled. "I wouldn't miss the grand announcement. Bet you a dollar your grandmother is going to brag she knew it was a girl all along, though I heard her tell your aunt yesterday she was sure it was a boy."

Hannah shook her head. "I'm not taking that sucker bet. Of course Mimi will claim to have known all along. That's what she does."

Pushing that near kiss to the back of his mind to analyze later, he placed a hand lightly at the center of her back and escorted her to the green cart. They would talk again later, he reminded himself. In the meantime, he needed to decide exactly what he wanted to say to her.

Not everyone in the family was waiting in the diner—at a swift glance, Hannah cataloged her uncle C.J., her cousin Lori and her grandfather among the missing—but the others all seemed to be waiting for her. She saw Shelby helping her mother behind the serving counter, an indication of how busy they'd been because Sarah usually handled grill and check-out duties on her own. Hannah's own mother had pitched in to wipe down tables, which meant someone else was running the store. Hannah hadn't thought to look that way when she'd entered the building. Was Lori at the store register? Or maybe Aaron, who wasn't here with the others? She'd heard he'd helped out in the store when Steven was hurt. Apparently her mother had been too impatient to wait there rather than in the grill with the rest of the family.

The family members not working in the diner were gathered around their usual big round table in the far corner. Maggie spotted Hannah and Andrew first, and motioned them over in excitement. "Well?" she called before they even had a chance to head that way.

Hannah wondered idly how many of her family's big events had played out in this little retro diner. Birthday cakes had been served here, announcements made, good and bad news received. While her family got along amazingly well considering how much time they spent together, her father and her uncle had once almost come to blows over a business dispute on a hot, harried afternoon and hadn't spoken for almost a week until Mimi had trapped them both in the grill and made them apologize to each other right in front of the customers. Growing up, Hannah had probably spent as many hours in this multipurpose building as she had in her parents' house. Along with her sister and cousins, she'd done her homework at the counter with mugs of hot chocolate on many a winter afternoon. Would her daughter sit at one of those high stools someday, kicking her feet and scribbling in a notebook?

Her mother reached her before anyone else, the table cleaning cloth dangling from one clenched hand. She searched Hannah's face. "Is everything okay?"

Hannah smiled reassuringly. "Everything is fine. Your granddaughter is developing perfectly."

Her mom caught her breath. "Granddaughter?" she asked in little more than a whisper. "It's a girl?"

"It's a girl," Hannah confirmed with a light laugh, one hand resting on her tummy.

Hugs and high fives ensued, and Hannah found herself fielding congratulations even from customers in the diner she'd never met before. The ultrasound picture was passed from hand to hand, examined and cooed over. Mimi, of course, declared loudly that she had known from the start that Hannah was carrying a girl because she had a knack for knowing those things. Because she was accustomed to her family's exuberance, Hannah wasn't particularly fazed by the outburst. As her father gave her a big hug, she noted that Andrew stood back quietly, cooperatively playing the part of her driver, nothing more. His own copy of the ultrasound photo was tucked discreetly out of sight.

She felt a pang of guilt, which wasn't helped when she heard her mother say to him, "You'll have to excuse us, Andrew. We're just so excited about the baby."

"I understand," Hannah heard him murmur in response. "I'm sure any family would be thrilled to anticipate the arrival of their first grandchild."

Hannah winced. And then noted that her sister was looking from her to Andrew and back again with speculative eyes.

"Shouldn't everyone get back to work?" Hannah asked, waving a hand around the busy diner. "We can talk later, after closing. Is Lori handling the desk?"

Her mother nodded. "Yes, Lori's at the desk and Aaron's running the store. He volunteered so I'd be free to meet you in here with everyone else. I should go relieve him."

"I was just headed back to my place," Maggie said, taking Hannah's arm. "You should put your feet up for a while, sis. Come on, I'll give you a ride."

"Oh, but there were a few things I was going to do this afternoon—" Hannah started to protest, but was immediately overridden by her concerned parents and grandmother, all of whom insisted she needed to go rest.

"Lori can finish up," Sarah agreed. "She needs to put in a few more hours this summer anyway. Heaven knows I'd rather see her helping us out than hanging around with Zach."

Outnumbered, Hannah surrendered. "Fine. I'll go put up my feet."

Maggie glanced at Andrew. "Need a ride back to Steven's?"

"No, thanks. I think I'll find my brother. I'll see you all later."

"Thank you for getting me to the doctor and helping me pick up my car," Hannah said to him for everyone else's benefit.

He gave her a look, but replied merely, "You're very welcome."

Maggie tugged at her hand. "Let's go. Sounds like it's starting to rain. Maybe if we hurry we can get inside again before the worst of it hits."

Knowing she would see Andrew later, Hannah turned to follow her sister out into the starting drizzle.

They dashed to the nearest cart parked in the reserved space beside the building and Maggie hopped behind the wheel. The rain started in earnest as she guided the cart onto the road, but the cart kept them mostly dry except for the occasional damp wind gust. Hannah didn't worry about it. She wouldn't melt if she got soaked.

"Thanks for the lift," she said when Maggie stopped the cart right at the foot of Hannah's steps.

"Oh, no, I'm coming in," Maggie insisted.

Hannah sighed. "Of course you are."

Chapter Five

The sisters dashed together through the now-pouring rain, crowding beneath the door's tiny overhang as Hannah shoved the key in her lock. Normally Maggie would have stood back to give her more room, maybe leaning against the railing of the redwood porch, but they were laughing and sticking close together to get what little protection they could from the downpour. They tumbled into the dry living room almost simultaneously. Hannah shook her head, sending raindrops flying. "Do you need a towel?"

"I didn't get that wet." Maggie pushed her hair out of her face and added, "I wouldn't turn down a cup of tea."

"Okay, put the kettle on. I'm going to change into dry clothes. The rain was blowing in my side of the cart."

She might have put on comfy pajamas had she not known Andrew would be coming by later. She settled for navy maternity yoga pants and a loose, pale blue cotton T-shirt with soft pink slippers. The tea was ready by the time she rejoined her sister. She accepted her mug with a murmured thank-you, letting the soothing scent of chamomile wash over her as she sank to the couch, feeling the stress of the day catching up to her. Knowing it wasn't over yet.

"So, did Andrew go in with you for the ultrasound?" Maggie asked from her chair, her mug cupped between her hands.

Hannah gazed into her tea to avoid meeting her sister's eyes. "Yes."

"How does he feel about having a daughter?"

Thinking of the expression in Andrew's eyes when he'd looked at the ultrasound monitor and then at her, Hannah looked up then. "He's thrilled."

"Wow." Hannah wasn't sure if Maggie was responding to the reply or to the implicit confirmation of her suspicion that Andrew really was the father.

Drawing a deep breath, Hannah nodded. "Yeah."

"Oh, my gosh." Maggie set down the cup, then pressed both hands to her cheeks. *"Andrew?"*

"Just as you suspected, I ran into him in Dallas last December. It— Well, things happened."

"So I see. And?"

"And what?"

Maggie gestured avidly with one hand, encouraging more detail. "Have you stayed in contact with him? How long has he known? When are you going to tell the family?"

"I haven't stayed in contact with him, he's known since he figured it out when Aaron mentioned in a phone call that I'm pregnant and we're telling the family this weekend. Probably."

Maggie hesitated a moment, then asked, "Does Mom know?"

"No." Hannah sighed. "I'm sorry I didn't tell you, Maggie. I wanted to. I just…didn't know who to tell first. It took me a while to wrap my head around what I'd done, and figure out what I was going to do about it."

Maggie nodded, apparently unsurprised by any of the decisions her sister had made. "I wish you'd felt comfortable talking with me, though. You had to feel very alone."

"I never felt alone," Hannah corrected her. "I knew the family was always here for me."

"Always will be."

"Yes, no matter how many bad decisions I make."

Maggie gave her a chiding look. "You haven't made that many."

Hannah snorted inelegantly. "Right."

Ever the loyal sister, Maggie insisted, "We all fell for Wade's act. I mean, he was never my favorite person, but I didn't know quite how horrible he was until after you had the sense to dump him. As for this—" she gestured vaguely toward Hannah's baby bump "—you've always wanted a baby, and you couldn't have chosen a better father."

Leave it to her determinedly optimistic sister to spin it that particular way, Hannah thought with a wry smile. Maybe she should have talked to Maggie from the beginning, rather than spending so much time brooding in self-recrimination. "I didn't exactly choose for Andrew to be the father of my child. It was an accident. Honestly, we thought we were being careful."

"Then it was just meant to be. So? How's it going to proceed from here? With you and Andrew, I mean."

"I'm not sure. We're going to talk later this evening. Try to make some decisions, I guess."

"I don't want to sound too much like Mimi—but you might as well be prepared for everyone to ask, so I'll start. Is there any chance that you and Andrew could maybe—"

"No," Hannah interrupted firmly, knowing exactly where this was headed. And her sister's automatic question was the most compelling reason Hannah had been so reluctant about telling her family. "That's not on the agenda."

"I see." Maggie kept her expression carefully neutral.

Thunder boomed outside, loud enough to rattle the windows in the trailer. The wind had picked up, too, and rain hammered against the roof and glass. It wasn't a severe storm, but Hannah hoped everyone in the resort was managing to stay safe and dry. She glanced at her watch. It was time for the marina, store and grill to close, so the rest of the family would be headed to their own homes soon unless they were waiting out the rain in the main building. "There's no need for you to go out in this deluge. Why don't we make some pasta or something for dinner?"

"Sounds like a plan," her sister agreed. "What time are you meeting Andrew?"

"We didn't really say. I guess he'll just show up later, maybe when the storm has passed."

Maggie nodded. "I'll give the two of you privacy when he gets here. But in the meantime, pasta sounds good."

They moved together toward the kitchen. Maggie

placed a hand on Hannah's arm when they reached the pantry. "Hannah?"

"Yes?"

"You know that no matter what happens, I'm always here for you and my niece, right?"

Touched, Hannah smiled. She thought fleetingly of all the squabbles and competitions and tiffs she and her sister had gotten into through the years, of all the times they'd fussed and pouted and tattled—and yet she was absolutely confident that Maggie meant every word of her promise. "I know, Mags. That goes both ways, you know."

"I know. Now, about that pasta…"

Because of the downpour, Andrew, Aaron and Steven lingered in the grill even after Sarah hung the Closed sign on the door. Shelby and her dad joined them a few minutes later, their own work finished for the day. Bryan and Linda had taken Mimi and Pop home in Bryan's dual-cab work truck, which he could drive straight into their garage to keep them from getting wet. Shelby's family decided to make a dinner of soup and sandwiches in the grill while waiting for the rain to stop. Andrew thought of Hannah, but they hadn't said anything about dining together, so he accepted Sarah's invitation for him to join them. He would slip over to Hannah's later.

"I wish Lori had waited until the storm passed to go out," Sarah fretted, glancing upward automatically when thunder boomed. "I don't like to think of her driving in this."

"You don't like to think of her driving in the rain to meet Zach," Shelby corrected.

C.J. scowled at the mention of his youngest child's undesirable boyfriend. Sarah hesitated, then nodded sheepishly. "I guess that has something to do with it."

Andrew had heard the family talk of Zach a few times during the past few days, enough for him to get the gist of why they didn't approve of him. "I know you said Lori's boyfriend got into some trouble as a juvenile, but is there any reason to believe he's living on the wrong side of the law now?" he asked, curious.

He watched as the family exchanged looks. "Not specifically," Sarah finally admitted. "He still looks like a delinquent, but as far as I know he hasn't been arrested lately."

"Do you want me to check into him? If there's genuine reason to be concerned about Lori spending time with the guy, I could probably find it."

Sarah's eyes went wide. "Can you do that? Legally, I mean?"

Andrew shrugged. "I can do a routine background check."

Aaron chuckled quietly. "He can do a bit more than that. Mostly legally, of course."

Andrew shot his brother a look, making Aaron grin unapologetically. Aaron, of course, was equally capable of running a background check, but Andrew could probably do so more quickly.

Shelby shook her head. "Lori would hate you for it."

"She wouldn't have to know," C.J. commented, looking thoughtful. "Not if Andrew doesn't find anything worrisome."

"You understand it would just be a surface check," Andrew warned. "I'm not going to follow him around and spy on him. I hardly think that's warranted, and

I don't have time anyway. I really have to be back in Dallas Monday."

As if to support his insistence, his phone chirped to announce a text message. Murmuring an apology to his dinner companions, he glanced at it, saw that it was a business question from one of his cousins who was working late at the agency and replied with a few quick thumb movements.

Lori's parents and brother all agreed that Andrew should run the check when he had time, though Shelby still looked doubtful. "It still seems sneaky to me. Lori would be angry and hurt."

"Maybe if someone had done this for Hannah she wouldn't have gotten tied up with Wade," C.J. murmured. "We'd have found out about all the secret debt Wade ran up before he married Hannah. Not to mention his tendency to sneak around with other women even when he was engaged to her. Would have spared that poor girl a truckload of heartache and saved the family a lot of trouble."

None of this was news to Andrew. He was the one who'd uncovered all that information—belatedly, of course. And while he would have given anything to have saved Hannah the pain she'd been through, if he hadn't been hired to help them resolve the issues with her ex, he never would have met her. He was beginning to understand what a great loss that would have been.

He scooped up another spoonful of the excellent beef vegetable soup Sarah had served him. "I'll let you know what I find out. Sarah, this soup is excellent."

Beaming, she jumped to her feet. "Let me get you some more."

"No, that's—"

But she was already in motion, snatching his mostly empty bowl from the table in front of him and heading for the counter.

Shelby grinned across the table at him, then glanced at Aaron. "Did you and Uncle Bryan get all the roof repairs done before the rain started?"

Aaron made a show of crossing his fingers. "I think so. As far as I know, no one has called to report a leak."

Aaron glanced at Andrew then. "The new security lights we ordered were delivered while you were gone with Hannah. We thought we'd start installing them tomorrow. The closed-circuit cameras will be in next week."

According to the security plans Andrew had drawn out and presented to Bryan, there would be three continuously running cameras installed at various points in the park. He'd actually recommended that measure last year, but it had taken Shelby's kidnapping to make them take that suggestion to heart. "Give me a call if you have any questions about my diagrams."

Aaron nodded. "We will."

Sarah set the refilled soup bowl in front of Andrew, then took her seat again. "Shelby, now that we know the baby's a girl, I'm going to start that quilt we discussed. Want to help me with it?"

"Of course. I think Hannah will stick with the sage and cream nursery colors she was considering, but we can add some touches of pink now."

"Pink for a girl? A little on the nose, isn't it?" Aaron teased her.

She dimpled at him. "Yes, but I happen to like pink for a baby girl. Doesn't mean I won't buy her a toy truck or teach her how to swing a bat later, of course."

Andrew wanted to be the one to teach his daughter to swing a bat. He wanted to share his awe at the thought of soon having a daughter to teach. He wanted to see how his brother's expression changed when he realized that Shelby's little cousin was also his niece. He wanted to tell his parents they were going to meet their first grandchild in a few months. But mostly, he realized, he wanted to be sitting with Hannah now rather than with this particular branch of the Bell family, as much as he liked them all.

He glanced at his watch, then toward the windows. The rain was still coming down, but not as heavily as before. By the time the meal was finished and cleared away, it was down to a drizzle. The family walked out beneath the outside awning, watching the rain while C.J. locked up behind them.

Leaning on his crutches, Steven drew a deep breath of rain-scented evening air. "Always liked the resort when it rains. Come late August, we'll be wishing for any drop of rain we can get."

Andrew could understand why Steven enjoyed the rain. Lights from the campgrounds glowed through the light rain like a misty watercolor painting. He imagined families gathered around tables in their campers or on the floors of their tents with cards and board games and snacks while listening to the drops hitting the roof. At least, that's what his family would have done.

"Your dad and I are going to run to town for a few things," Sarah said to Steven and Shelby. "Anyone need us to pick up anything?"

Andrew wasn't surprised they were going supplies shopping late on a Friday evening, probably at the twenty-four-hour superstore some fifteen miles away.

With the long hours they put in at the resort this time of year, this would be the only time both were free to leave for a couple hours. He knew they could have had someone shop for them, but they would probably enjoy getting away for a bit, even if just to grocery shop. The families took vacations each year during the off-season, closing the resort for a week in December and another in February, but there was no getting away during the summer, especially with a long holiday weekend rapidly approaching.

He thought guiltily of his own piling-up responsibilities back at his office, but pushed the concern to the back of his mind for now. His company's mantra had always been Family First—and he was definitely here for family reasons.

He drove Steven back to the trailer in the golf cart. The rain had completely stopped by the time he turned onto the private drive leading into the family compound. Water splashed from shallow puddles beneath the wheels as he drove through the dark stretch of road just beyond the sign. Within a few days, this area would be well-lit, which would make him feel somewhat better about leaving Hannah here.

Eh, what was he thinking? Nothing was going to make that parting any easier.

As soon as they were inside, Steven went back to his bedroom to start his nightly crunches, curls and other exercises to keep himself in shape while he recuperated from his accident. Having mentioned that he would take a long walk to enjoy the rain-cooled evening, Andrew let himself out, locking the door behind him. The family compound was well-lit, so he'd have been visible crossing the road to Hannah's place if anyone had been watching, but he saw no one else around. Lights burned in Maggie's house, and he thought he saw the flicker of a television through the slats in the living room blinds. Aaron was closed in with Shelby, and Andrew figured his brother was pleasantly occupied.

So why did he have the sudden, strange feeling that he was being watched? Pausing on Hannah's porch with one hand resting lightly on the railing, he looked around with narrowed eyes, but saw nothing suspicious. Despite the lighting, there were scattered shadows where someone could hide, especially if dressed in dark clothing, but he saw nothing that made him feel compelled to go investigate. Across the street, he saw Pax sleeping contentedly on Steven's porch. Not that the dog was a reliable guard, but he seemed to have no concerns.

Shaking his head, he told himself he was letting paranoia carry him away. He supposed Hannah's near obsession about secrecy was affecting him more than he'd realized. True, it wasn't like him—his instincts were usually almost uncannily reliable—but then nothing about the past few days had been normal for him.

Drawing a deep breath, he tapped on the door. A moment later, it opened. Her serene expression belied by the nerves apparent in her eyes, Hannah moved aside. "Come in, Andrew. I've been waiting for you."

Automatically, Hannah scanned the grounds after letting Andrew in. She wasn't sure why she felt compelled to do so; maybe it was to see if anyone was around to have watched him enter. Maybe because seeing her ex-husband's father again earlier—especially not long before picking up her vandalized car—had left her jumpy and hypervigilant. Maybe because her upcoming talk with Andrew made her nervous and she was projecting that anxiety outside.

She closed the door, then smoothed her hands down her T-shirt before turning to face him. "Have you eaten? Maggie and I had pasta, but there are leftovers in the fridge."

"Thanks, but I ate with Aaron and Shelby and her family."

"Was Lori there?"

He shook his head. "She left after work. Your aunt Sarah wasn't happy about Lori going out in the worst of the rainstorm."

"I have a feeling it wasn't the rain my aunt was unhappy about."

He shrugged because they both knew that was true. Hannah wished she could have done more to warn her young cousin about the dangers inherent with getting involved with the wrong man. But then, she didn't know for certain whether Zach was a decent guy or not. Other than his wild reputation in aimless local gossip, she knew little about him. It was obvious that Lori resented any unwanted advice about her love life. Hannah might have felt the same way had anyone tried to warn her about Wade all those years ago, though he'd been so good at conning people that everyone had thought he was just wonderful.

Thinking of how perfect Wade had pretended to be made her even more worried about getting involved with Andrew. Practically perfect-in-every-way Andrew, the hero of her family—well, until his twin brother had heroically saved her cousin's life. Now he was more like a co-hero. She didn't think he deliberately misrepresented himself, of course. Unlike her ex, Andrew was exactly what he appeared to be. Practically perfect. Why did that seem to be almost as insurmountable an obstacle as Wade's duplicity?

"What are you thinking about so seriously?" he asked her, tilting his head as he studied her face. She realized she'd been standing in front of the door for several minutes, lost in her rather incoherent thoughts.

She moved away from the door into the room. "You wouldn't understand."

"Try me."

Instead, she walked toward the couch, avoiding his eyes. "Maggie and I watched the news while we ate. Sounds as though the rain is over. The rest of the weekend is supposed to be beautiful weather-wise. We needed the rain, but I'm sure our guests are happy with the forecast."

He stepped in front of her so that she had no option but to look at him. "We're talking about the weather now?"

His quiet question made her wince. "Just making small talk."

"I think we're past that, don't you?"

She pushed a hand through her hair. "I just…"

Having no clue how she'd planned to finish that sentence, she fell silent.

Andrew raised a hand to skim the line of her jaw with his fingertips, gliding across her cheek and then pausing to trace her lower lip. Just a brush of his hand—and yet she felt as though she had been thoroughly kissed. Perhaps it was the look in his eyes as he gazed so intently at her mouth. Maybe it was just the reawakening of memories she tried so hard and so often to suppress.

"I don't want you to be afraid of me, Hannah," he said quietly, resting his hand against her cheek.

She sighed, covering his hand with her own. "I'm not afraid of you, Andrew. Maybe I'm a little afraid of myself when I'm around you."

It was an unguarded admission, and maybe she shouldn't have let it slip, but something in his expression made her think he completely understood. He lifted his other hand to cup her face between his palms, and then he brushed his lips over hers. Perhaps he'd intended it only as a reassuring caress, a sweet moment of bonding. Maybe he didn't plan for it to go any further, or to evolve into anything more than a light kiss. If so, he'd forgotten to account for the sparks that seemed to fly whenever their lips met, or the fires those sparks ignited.

The kiss changed, deepened. His hands fell, his arms going around her to pull her closer. There was a momentary hesitation when their bodies met, as they adjusted for her changed shape, and Hannah started to draw back. But then Andrew's hands made a slow sweep down her back and the tip of his tongue traced her lower lip before slipping inside her mouth. The heat rose, spreading rapidly from her mouth to her limbs to a place deep inside her heart that had been cold and dark since the morning she'd said goodbye to him for what she'd thought had been the last time.

Her arms were around his neck. When had that happened? Her sensitive breasts brushed against his solid chest, reminding her of how very good he looked and felt beneath the conservative clothes he favored. His thighs were rock solid when they tangled with her legs.

He was aroused and hungry, and his kisses left no doubt of that.

She pulled her mouth from his, drawing in a deep, unsteady breath, her hands clutching his shoulders for support.

Andrew smiled down at her somewhat apologetically. "Did I get carried away? Sorry. December was a long time ago."

Surely he wasn't implying that he hadn't—

"There hasn't been anyone since," he said as if reading the question in her eyes. "I've been really busy and traveled a lot and...well, there just wasn't anyone else I wanted to be with."

Had he thought of her during those months? Could she possibly have crossed his mind as often as he had hers?

She couldn't stop herself from flashing back to that morning when she'd awoken in his arms before dawn, opening her eyes to see his sleeping face on the pillow next to hers. There had been very little light in her hotel room, but she'd had no trouble seeing his relaxed features. Perhaps because they were so strongly imprinted in her mind.

She had panicked. It was the only word to describe the sudden, throat-closing, heart-stopping fear that had gripped her in response to seeing him there. In response to her own momentary jolt of sheer happiness at waking beside him. She couldn't allow herself to feel that way, she'd immediately told herself, furiously. She would not allow her happiness to be dependent again on any man. Wade had burned her, but she suspected that Andrew had the power to reduce her to ashes. A wise woman would send him away. She'd wanted to believe that experience had brought her a measure of wisdom—despite one night of reckless weakness.

Slipping from the bed, she'd wrapped herself in a robe, closing it to the throat and tightly knotting the belt. "Andrew," she'd said too sharply.

His eyes had immediately opened, without visible confusion or disorientation. "Yes?"

"You need to go."

She had watched his eyebrows knit, the shadows concealing the expression in his eyes. "What time is it?"

"Late. Or early, I guess. I'm meeting my college friends for breakfast before I head back to the resort. I'd like some time to myself to get dressed and packed."

Andrew studied her a moment before climbing from the bed. She'd averted her eyes when he reached for his clothes, afraid that the sight of his naked perfection would weaken her resolve. He dressed quickly, then circled the bed to stand in front of her. "I'm sure you need a little time to process this," he'd said, his voice so gentle and understanding that a lump had formed in her throat. "I'll call you in a few days."

"No," she'd quickly said, hoarsely. She'd swallowed, then continued more steadily. "It would be better if you didn't, really. The holidays are going to be very busy, and after that we'll start gearing up for the busy season at the resort and I—"

"Hannah." He'd silenced her with his fingertips on her lips. "I wasn't looking for a one-night stand with you."

He'd probably thought the reassurance would allay her fears. Instead, it had only made her more nervous.

"That's all I have to offer," she had answered him simply, drawing on all her strength to directly meet his eyes. "I want—I need to be on my own now, to focus on myself, my job, my family. Last night was great, Andrew, but let's just leave it at that, shall we? A pleasant memory."

And then, like a fool, she'd offered her right hand to him for a shake, a memory that still embarrassed her as she stood in his arms now, her lips still tingling from his kisses. Her face heated, both in response to those painful memories and the feelings being roused in her again tonight.

Andrew studied her with narrowed eyes, trying to read the expressions that must have flitted over her face in the past few moments. Did he remember that awkwardly extended hand, the way he'd looked in disbelief from her face to her hand and back again before turning toward the door without touching her? He'd let himself out after telling her she knew where to find him if she ever needed him. She had spent the hours until sunrise sitting in an uncomfortable chair and wondering if the hurt she'd seen in his eyes had been because of wounded male pride, or if she had truly disappointed him when she'd sent him away so unceremoniously.

Despite her request, he'd tried to call a time or two afterward, but she had neither answered nor returned his calls. Cowardly and rather rude, perhaps, but she'd needed the distance...especially after the shock of finding herself pregnant. The fact that he'd been with no other woman since—and Andrew was nothing if not truthful—had her wondering all over again what that night had meant to him. Her confusion only reinforced that she still couldn't think coherently where Andrew was involved.

He drew a deep breath, making her aware of how

long she'd stood there without saying anything since he'd admitted she'd been the last woman he'd been with. Brushing his lips lightly over the tip of her nose, he then stepped back. "You asked me here to talk. I promise to behave myself now."

How ridiculous was it that she was rather disappointed to hear him say that? Smiling wryly at her own folly, she shook her head. "You've always befuddled me, Andrew. How do you do that?"

He laughed softly. "Befuddled?"

She shrugged. "Seems like a fitting description. When I'm around you, I can't seem to think clearly, which makes me wonder what you think of me. Despite the turmoil that always seems to surround me when you're here, I really am an intelligent and competent woman."

"Surely you don't believe I have any doubt of that," he said with one raised eyebrow. "I certainly don't think any less of you because of your ex-husband's actions. I admire you for kicking him to the curb as soon as you became aware of his true nature, and for cooperating so fully last year in my investigation, even when you felt obliged to tell me things you understandably wanted to keep private. As for our current situation—" he motioned vaguely toward her midsection "—I'm as responsible for this as you are, if not more so. I thought I was taking adequate precautions."

"Accidents happen," she murmured, resting a hand on her tummy.

He nodded. "I know."

But they didn't usually happen to him, she added silently.

Her hand still resting over their daughter, she lifted

her chin and met his eyes. "I want you to know I don't regret this. This child will be greeted with love and joy, and raised to be proud of her family and her heritage."

"I don't regret it either," he replied just as firmly. "Maybe we didn't plan this, but I consider it a blessing rather than a mistake. We love kids in my family. I've always imagined myself as being a dad someday, though it was always in some vague future."

And with some other woman? she thought wistfully.

"Anyway," he continued, "that's why you asked me over, right? To talk about how we proceed from here."

She nodded. "We have a lot of decisions to make."

"We do, but the first and most important decision concerns us. Which brings me to a proposition I have for you."

He cleared his throat, looking suddenly, uncharacteristically nervous. Her heart suddenly pounding against her chest, Hannah felt her eyes widen. Surely he wasn't going to suggest...

"Hannah, would you—"

A hard thump on the back of the trailer made him whirl in that direction with a frown. "What on earth?"

She must have jumped a foot in response to the crash, which only demonstrated how much she had tensed when Andrew started to speak. He crossed the room to draw back the curtain and look out the back window into the darkness.

"Do you see anything?" she asked. "Is it still raining? Is the wind blowing?"

"No to all of the above." He turned toward the door. "Maybe a tree limb fell?"

"There isn't a tree behind my house," she reminded

him. "Not close enough for a limb to hit without any wind anyway."

"Stay here. I'll check it out, just to be safe." He reached for the doorknob, shaking his head. "We really are going to finish this conversation eventually."

She was sure he meant it as a promise rather than a threat. So it made no sense that she gulped and wiped her suddenly damp palms on her yoga pants in response.

She stood in the open doorway while Andrew walked around the end of her home to investigate the sound. The air still felt cool and damp against her face. Overhead, the clouds were beginning to drift apart, revealing patches of stars sprinkled in the night sky. Puddles on the asphalt road reflected the light from the security lamps on tall poles between the mobile homes. Across the road, she saw Pax snoozing on Steven's porch, his stocky yellow body illuminated by the amber porch light burning beside the front door. Poor old Pax was going to miss Steven when he left for the fire academy. The dog would be well-cared for and would get plenty of attention from the rest of the affectionate family, but he and Steven shared a special bond.

She made a mental note to give the dog a little extra attention herself in the fall, then remembered that she would have a newborn infant by then. She swallowed hard again. Every once in a while, the reality of that huge looming change in her life overwhelmed her.

Speaking of imminent challenges...

Andrew came back into view, shrugging when he met her eyes. "I didn't see anything."

"That's odd. I wonder what made that noise?"

"I'll look again tomorrow in daylight," he promised,

coming up the steps. He paused when he reached the top. She didn't immediately move out of the doorway.

"Well?" he asked. "Are you going to let me in?"

"I'm thinking about it," she admitted, resting one hand against the doorjamb. She would let him in, of course, but considering where their conversation had seemed to be headed earlier, she didn't think anyone could blame her for procrastinating.

Wearing a faint smile, Andrew crossed his arms and leaned back against the railing. "Is there a password or—"

She heard a loud crack and she cried out in shock when Andrew fell backward, disappearing from in front of her eyes.

Chapter Six

Rousing herself from her momentary paralysis, Hannah leaped forward. Andrew lay on the ground on his back, surrounded by broken segments of the redwood handrailing from her porch. Taking as much care as possible, she hurried down the still-slightly damp steps.

Andrew was already struggling to rise on one elbow when she reached him. His face was thrown into shadows, but she thought she saw a dark smear on his forehead. She touched her fingers to his face, and they came away sticky. "You're bleeding."

"Bumped my head on a rock," he muttered, tentatively raising his hand to his temple. "It's just a graze."

"Don't move, I'll call for help."

He caught her wrist when she would have moved away. "Hannah, it was a three-foot fall. I'll be fine."

Still, he'd fallen hard, landing awkwardly on rocks

and the broken railing. She hovered nearby when he rose gingerly. Before he'd even made it all the way to his feet, she heard doors open and raised voices.

"Is everything okay?" Maggie called from next door.

Aaron must have looked out from across the road to check on the noise. He sprinted over to support his brother, taking in the scene in a sweeping glance as Shelby followed only a bit more slowly. Aaron was still in jeans and a T-shirt, bare feet stuffed into sandals. Shelby wore plaid sleep shorts, a lace-edged tank top and flip-flops, evidence to Hannah that they'd settled in for a quiet evening. Pax raised his head from Steven's porch and gave a questioning bark.

"Everything okay over there?" Steven called from his doorway.

"It's fine, Steven," Andrew replied. "Don't try to get out. We're good."

"Andrew, you're bleeding," Shelby said, peering up at him.

He swiped at his temple with the back of one hand, smearing blood across his cheek, a dark stripe in the dim light. "It's shallow," he assured them. "I'll stick an adhesive strip on it in a minute. First, I want to know what happened with this railing. How the hell did it break just from my leaning against it?"

"Good question," Aaron agreed grimly, bending to study the broken rail. "Hannah, do you have a flashlight?"

"I'll get it," Maggie said before Hannah could reply, heading toward the door. "I know where she keeps it."

Hannah figured Maggie thought she could move faster and more safely up the steps—and she was probably right. Maggie was back in only a couple of minutes while Hannah hovered close to Andrew, her throat still tight from the shock of watching him fall. She noted that he moved rather stiffly as he and Aaron closely examined the railing and the porch, talking in low, solemn voices while Aaron ran the beam of the flashlight over every inch of wood on the ground and the porch. Andrew's white shirt and khaki pants were smeared with mud now—at least, she hoped it was only mud and that there wasn't any blood hidden by the dirt.

"I can't imagine why that railing broke," Maggie fretted, shaking her head. "Dad built that porch himself, and he's such a stickler about making sure everything is solid and secure."

"The broken railing was a result of Andrew's fall, not the cause of it," Aaron replied grimly.

Hannah frowned. "I don't understand."

Andrew rested a hand on her shoulder. Even though his touch was gentle, his face was hard with barely suppressed anger. "Someone deliberately sabotaged your railing, Hannah. Some of the wood screws are missing altogether, and I know your dad didn't leave it that way. When I leaned against the railing, the supports gave way. The handrail broke when I landed on it."

Hannah was stunned into silence. Not so Maggie. "Who on earth would take the screws out of Hannah's porch?" she asked in bewilderment. "And why?"

"I'll be right back." Carrying the flashlight, Aaron ran next door to Maggie's trailer, where he examined the porch closely before crossing the road to Shelby's and Steven's homes.

Seeing Andrew wipe his face again, Hannah shook off her stupor. "Come inside," she ordered him. "I want to get a look at that cut. I have a first-aid kit if it only needs a bandage. I can make tea for anyone who wants to come in for some."

Shelby glanced down as if trying to decide if her state of dress was sufficient, then shrugged and nodded. "Tea sounds good. I'm sure the guys are going to want to talk about this."

Thinking of a talk that had been delayed—yet again—Hannah nodded and turned toward her home, accepting her sister's help as they climbed the steps.

Andrew was furious and having a hard time keeping that anger in check. He did not consider himself a violent man, but if the person who had removed the screws from Hannah's porch supports stood in front of him now, he couldn't promise he would keep his hands to himself. The thought of her falling, hitting the ground with the same force he had, especially in her condition—the thought of her being injured, maybe even losing the baby…

His fists clenched and a low growl escaped his tight throat.

Hannah's hands stilled in the process of cleaning and bandaging the cut at his left temple. "Am I hurting you?"

She and Maggie had both fussed that perhaps he should go to the E.R. for a scan, but he'd assured them that wasn't necessary and Aaron had backed him up. He was sore all over and figured he'd have more than a few colorful bruises the next day. There was a distinct possibility he'd cracked a rib on his right side. A dull headache throbbed in his temples and at the back of his neck, but his vision was fine, he wasn't dizzy or confused. He wasn't concussed, just mad as hell.

"You aren't hurting me. Just stick a bandage on it and I'll be fine."

Leaning over the kitchen chair in which he sat, she frowned at him. "If you won't be still, the bandage is liable to end up in your eye."

Sitting across the table with a cup of hot tea, Shelby giggled. Andrew gave her a look, but subsided so Hannah could finish her task.

Not amused, Aaron paced the kitchen. "So no one's porch was touched except Hannah's," he murmured, organizing his thoughts aloud. "We haven't had time to check the houses, but there's no reason to think anything has been done there. We should check in daylight tomorrow, just to be sure, but this seems to be aimed at Hannah for some reason. Which makes the slashing of her tires yesterday look less like a random act of vandalism."

Unable to stay away, Steven had crossed the road on his crutches to join them. He sat now at the table with Maggie and Shelby, all of them watching Aaron pace and Hannah patch Andrew's cut. "Who would want to hurt Hannah of all people? I mean, Hannah's the nicest of all of us."

Andrew noted that Maggie and Shelby nodded as if that were a given, while Hannah made an embarrassed sound of skepticism.

Aaron turned to cock his head in Steven's direction. "Is there any chance sabotage was involved in your accident?" he asked, nodding toward the crutches propped at the back of Steven's chair.

Steven shook his head. "Totally my own fault. I let my thoughts wander while I was mowing, took an angle too steeply and turned over the mower."

Even though Steven didn't further elaborate, Andrew figured he'd been thinking about his future, trying to work up the courage to tell his family he wanted to leave the resort and train for a firefighting career.

"So it's aimed at Hannah, then," Aaron said with a grim expression.

Andrew felt the slightest tremor in Hannah's fingers when she smoothed the adhesive bandage against his temple. Once again fury flared, and again he had to forcefully tamp it down. He needed to think clearly, rationally, and he couldn't do that when his mind was clouded with anger.

Maggie watched Hannah pack away the first-aid supplies. "Chuck Cavender," she said simply.

Hannah started. "We can't know that."

Andrew remembered that her ex-father-in-law had been the first person who'd popped into Hannah's mind as a potential suspect in the vandalism of her car. He remembered, too, the uneasy feeling he'd had when they'd all ended up at the same intersection earlier that day.

He stood to push Hannah gently but firmly into his chair at the four-seat table, saying she needed to get off her feet for a while. "Does he resent you that much?" he asked when she was settled.

"Yes," she said simply. "But it still seems unlike him to sneak around and cause this kind of mischief."

"This was more than mischief, Hannah. This was an attack on you and the baby," Andrew snapped, his simmering temper momentarily getting away from him. He wasn't angry with her of course, but it was a good thing Chuck Cavender wasn't within his reach at that moment. "I think I'll have a talk with him tomorrow."

Hannah swiveled in the chair to gaze up at him. "Andrew, you can't just show up at his house and throw accusations at him without some sort of evidence. You of all people should know that."

"I know how to question a suspect." Aware that he'd snapped, he grimaced somewhat apologetically afterward.

She narrowed her eyes at him, reading the emotions roiling inside him. "With your fists?"

"If necessary."

"I can see how Cavender could have gotten to your tires," Aaron mused, leaning against the counter. "But would it be so easy for him to get to your porch? He'd have had to come through the gate, right?"

"Well, anyone can come through the gate," Maggie pointed out. "If they aren't registered guests, all they have to do is pay five dollars for one day's admission."

And no names or license plate numbers were taken at the gate, Andrew thought. Maybe that should change in the future.

"Still, he'd have risked being recognized by someone," Aaron continued. "I'm assuming he spent some time here when you and the evil ex were married, Hannah."

She nodded with a grimace at his use of the nickname everyone in the family had given Wade.

"He wouldn't necessarily have come through the gate," Steven suggested.

Leaning side by side against the counter now, Andrew and Aaron both looked hard at Hannah's cousin. "There's another way in?" Andrew asked. "Why didn't I know that?"

"The old road?" Maggie asked, looking from Steven to Hannah. "I guess Wade knew about it, but would Chuck?"

"I don't know," Hannah replied unhappily.

"What old road?" Andrew demanded.

"It's hardly more than a dirt path through the woods now," Steven explained. "It's the original road from the old highway to the river, before the dam was put in and the resort was built. It's not on any of our resort maps, but it runs through the woods behind Pop and Mimi's house. We used to ride four-wheelers and dirt bikes on the road when we were kids, but it's pretty rutted and overgrown now. It's still accessible from the old highway, though there's a chain and a No Trespassing sign at the entrance. I guess someone could have gotten around the chain if they set their mind to it."

Andrew was stunned that he'd never known about the old road. "Why the hell didn't anyone tell me about that road? Did anyone mention it to you?" he asked Aaron.

His brother shook his head. "First I've heard of it."

"Not even when Shelby was missing?" Andrew asked in exasperation. "You didn't search it then to see if the chain was still in place?"

"Aaron didn't know about it and the rest of us didn't think of it," Maggie admitted. "Besides, Aaron was pretty sure he knew who had Shelby, so his focus was on Cabin 7."

Andrew slammed a hand down on the counter in frustration. "So I've been focusing on a plan for lighting and closed-circuit cameras without even knowing there was an unsecured entrance to the damn resort?"

He was aware that everyone except his brother was looking at him in surprise. Aaron was more accustomed to seeing Andrew's rare but occasionally explosive bursts of temper.

"We've never really had any serious problems here before," Shelby explained tentatively. "I mean, sure, we've had to summon the police a few times for drunk-and-disorderly calls. The evil ex caused us all that trouble last summer, but he didn't sneak into the resort in the process. Even when Landon—or whatever his real name was—grabbed me, it was a stupid and impulsive act, not a well-planned, covert operation. The old road just never crossed our minds."

"I want a topographical map of this place. I want to know every possible way in or out, even if it's just a footpath."

Hannah studied Andrew with a raised eyebrow in response to his imperious commands. "You are aware that you aren't on the job here, right?"

He leveled a look at her. "Let's just say I have a vested interest in keeping this family safe."

Maggie coughed.

Shelby smiled weakly at Aaron. "Is he this protective of all his former clients?"

"Not so much," Aaron murmured, his expression suddenly speculative.

"I will find out who's behind this," Andrew promised. "If it's Cavender, I'll find proof, and I'll put a stop to it."

"You have to be back in Dallas Monday," Hannah reminded him.

"I'm in, too," Aaron said immediately. "I'll help you investigate and keep an eye on Hannah when you aren't here."

Feeling torn between his responsibilities in Dallas

and his concern about Hannah and the baby, Andrew nodded shortly.

"Should we call the police about what happened tonight?" Shelby asked.

Even as he glanced at Andrew for confirmation, Aaron was shaking his head. "There's nothing really to report. Without evidence that there was actual sabotage to the porch, they'll say it's just as likely the screws were left out in construction."

Maggie scowled. "Our dad would never—"

"He said we need proof," Hannah cut in to remind her sister. "If there's a way to prove who did this, Andrew will find it."

Even though gratified by her confidence, Andrew was still on edge. He was relieved that the others left not long afterward, Maggie declaring that Andrew probably had some questions for Hannah and then Hannah needed to rest. The way Maggie looked at him as she rushed his brother and her cousins out made him wonder if she either knew or suspected his role in Hannah's pregnancy. He watched Aaron and Shelby help Steven across the road, then closed the door and turned back to Hannah.

He wasn't sure what he expected her to say, but it wasn't "Okay, now that everyone is gone, take off your shirt."

He lifted an eyebrow. "I beg your pardon?"

She advanced on him with a frown of determination. "I know you didn't want to make a big deal of your fall in front of the others, but I've seen the way you wince every time you turn sideways. I want to see the damage."

"I'm okay, Hannah. Bruised and a little sore, but I wasn't really hurt."

Her hands were already working at the top button of his now-dirty white shirt. "Take it off."

Sighing, he covered her hands with his. "This isn't exactly the way I'd hoped to hear you say this."

Her mouth twitched with the hint of a smile, but she didn't let him distract her that easily. "I just want to make sure you're really okay, Andrew."

He couldn't argue with the genuine concern in her liquid emerald eyes. Resigned, he nodded and completed the task, himself, stripping the shirt away. Her intake of breath confirmed his suspicion that he bore a few scrapes and bruises from the fall. She reached out to brush her fingertips very lightly over his left side. Even though she barely touched him, he felt the tenderness of the skin there.

"You have a bad scrape here," she said, her voice not entirely steady, though she was obviously trying to mask her emotions. "It bled a little. Let me clean it up and put some ointment on it. Do you think the rib is broken?"

"Cracked maybe," he replied honestly, keeping his tone gentle. "Not the first time I've cracked a rib. I'll be okay, Hannah."

She kept her eyes on the scrape as she drew a long breath. "I can't tell you how scared I was when you fell. You just…disappeared in front of my eyes. I was so afraid you were…"

"It was a three-foot drop," he reminded her again. "I know how to take a fall, which kept me from being seriously hurt. I couldn't avoid the broken railing or bumping my head on that one rock. I'm just glad I'm the one who fell and not you."

She moistened her lips. "Usually I hang on to the railing when I climb the stairs these days for safety reasons. I didn't this evening because it was raining and I crowded close to the awning to stay dry. Maggie was with me and she gave me a hand."

His stomach clenched again at the thought of what could have happened, but he pushed the images out of his mind. Or tried to. "You should put your feet up again. You've had a very long day."

"No kidding," she said, pushing a hand through her hair.

"Actually, why don't you go on to bed," he suggested. He didn't like seeing the purple shadows developing beneath her eyes. Today alone she had worked, had a doctor's appointment, shared the amazing ultrasound experience with him, then found out that someone was targeting her with escalating menace. No wonder she looked wiped-out. She certainly wasn't ready to discuss the future with him, especially the future he was prepared to suggest to her. "We'll talk tomorrow, after you've rested."

She took his hand and gave a little tug. "Come with me."

Both his eyebrows shot up that time. "Um—"

"I want to treat that scrape," she reminded him. "After that you can go back to Steven's."

Carrying his shirt, he accompanied her through her bedroom and into the attached bath. He paid little attention to decor other than to note that the bedroom was tidy, big enough for a queen-size bed and a nightstand in addition to a closet and built-in storage drawers and

vanity table, and that the palette was as neutral as the
rest of her comfortable, but rather impersonal, home.
It occurred to him that it seemed a bit out of character
for Hannah to have so little color in her home. True,
it was a mobile home with somewhat limited decorating potential, but Shelby had bedecked hers with a riot
of colors, while Steven's place was personalized in the
colors of his favorite sports team. He hadn't been inside Maggie's place, but he doubted it would be quite
so impersonal. He was no shrink, but he'd like to know
more about why Hannah had avoided committing to any
specific colors in her surroundings.

She took a washcloth from a cabinet and wetted it
in the sink, adding a squirt of liquid soap. "I'll try not
to hurt you, but I'd like to clean up some of that dried
blood to see if you need a bandage."

"You won't hurt me." Still, he flinched when she
pressed the cloth to his skin. "Not pain," he assured
her with a wry chuckle. "It's cold."

Hannah looked at him apologetically. "Sorry. Guess
I should have let the water warm a bit."

"It's fine." He was actually warming up quickly as
she bent over to focus on his bare side. A strand of her
hair brushed his stomach and the muscles there con-
tracted instinctively. He shifted his weight on his feet,
hoping she didn't notice that his body was reacting in
a wholly male way to her ministrations.

"I don't think it needs a bandage," she pronounced
after another uncomfortable couple of minutes. "It's just
a scrape on the surface. There's some swelling and dis-
coloration, though. Maybe you should have an X-ray?"

He shook his head. "Even if the rib is cracked, there's

nothing to be done about it except wait for it to heal. I'll take some ibuprofen later for the inflammation."

She turned him around and grumbled about the bruises on his back, but apparently decided there was nothing more she could do for them. Instead, she dug out a bottle of ibuprofen and shook out a couple for him to take. He tossed them into his mouth and swallowed them dry. "Thanks."

She turned toward the doorway. "I'll get you a glass of water. Then I'll lock up behind you after you leave."

He caught her arm to detain her. She wasn't going to like what he had to say next. "You won't have to lock up behind me. I'm not going anywhere tonight."

Hannah stared at Andrew for a moment with narrowed eyes, wondering if she had heard him correctly. "What did you say?"

He didn't look notably discouraged by her tone. "I told Steven I'm sleeping in your guest room tonight— or on your couch if there's no bed in your guest room. I'm going to run over for clean clothes later, but I'm not leaving you alone here until we figure out who's been harassing you and put a stop to it."

She was suddenly intensely aware of him being in her private bath in a way she hadn't been when she'd focused on his injuries. She moistened her lips before saying, "There's no need for you to stay here. I'll lock the doors, and you'll be right across the road anyway. There's no reason to believe I'm in any danger. It's not as though I've been physically attacked."

"What would you call this?" he demanded, motioning vaguely toward the bandage on his face. "I got some bruises and a bump on the head, but what if you had taken that fall?"

Automatically her hand went to her stomach. She'd pictured that possibility too many times—not for fear of what might have happened to her, but to their child. She felt guilty for being relieved Andrew had taken the fall rather than her, even knowing he would risk anything to protect her and the baby. That was just the kind of man he was. She was so very glad he hadn't been seriously injured.

"I'm not leaving you unprotected until I know you're safe," he said flatly. "You can ask me to leave and I will, but I'll just spend the night sitting on your porch."

She sighed impatiently. "Fine. I have a spare bedroom at the other end of the trailer, but the bed in there is only a twin size. You're too tall to fit comfortably on it. I'll take that bed. You can have mine."

"I'll take the guest bed. You stay in your own. You need a good night's rest."

Hannah planted her hands on her hips to glare at him. "Are you going to let me win any argument tonight?"

"Well, if you argued that I should share your bed with you, you could probably convince me...."

He couldn't know how tempting it was for her to do just that. "Um—"

He chuckled, though he looked more weary than genuinely amused. "I'm teasing, Hannah. Get some sleep. We'll try to figure everything out tomorrow."

She didn't know how well she would sleep while her mind whirled with everything awaiting her tomorrow. Andrew, her family, the reality that someone hated her enough to plan these cowardly assaults against her. Not to mention her awareness that Andrew would be sleeping in the guest room only a few yards away. She would probably spend an hour or so wondering if he had only been joking about sharing her bed—and the rest of the night trying to convince herself she'd been right not to follow up on that suggestion.

Even splotched with darkening bruises, his bare chest was so appealing that it was all she could do to keep her hands off him. There was no question that he kept himself in excellent condition. He was lean and strong and sleek, the kind of body a woman could happily run her hands over for hours. She knew that from experience.

"There's no need to look so distressed," he said, cupping her face between his hands to gaze into her eyes. "I know it's been a crazy few days, and I know you have to be concerned about what happened tonight, but we'll sort everything out after you get some rest. I just want to make sure nothing else happens tonight to disturb your sleep. You know you have nothing to worry about from me."

"I think I told you earlier that I'm not afraid of you," she murmured, covering his left hand with her right. "It's myself I don't trust when you're around."

He brushed his lips across hers, just a taste of the kiss she craved. "I can't deny I'm delighted that I have that effect on you, especially because I feel very much the same way when you're in the same room with me. But I'm here to take care of you, Hannah. I won't give you a reason to regret having me here."

She frowned in response to the words he'd intended as reassuring. "I don't need anyone taking care of me, Andrew. Not even you."

He winced. "That didn't come out exactly the way I intended."

She shook off his hands, drawing herself up to her full height. "Maybe I've made some mistakes—and I guess I can't blame you for doubting my competence, considering that you always seem to rush to my rescue—but I assure you I can take care of myself and my child. I was the one who ended my travesty of a marriage even when Wade tried to manipulate me into staying with him. Yes, I'm living at the family resort, but I'm doing a job I trained to do—and handling it well, I might add. I live in a trailer, but it's one I bought and am paying for myself. With the exception of the salary I earn, I take no money from my family."

"Hannah—"

"And I don't need you protecting me from myself either," she continued forcefully. "If I decide I want to kiss you, you don't need to stop me for my own good!"

He looked suitably cowed as he held up his hands in surrender. "I'm sorry. I didn't mean to imply that you need me to—well, for anything, really."

She growled low in her throat, as annoyed with herself as with him. Those crazy pregnancy hormones had just kicked in again. And he was still standing there, battered and bare-chested, so determined to protect her, looking so chagrined for having upset her.

Before she was even aware of moving, she had her arms around him, her mouth pressed to his. Despite his promises to exert willpower, Andrew made no effort to push her away. Instead, he gathered her against him, returning the kiss with a heat and fervor that only intensified her own passion. If the embrace caused him any discomfort, he either ignored it or didn't notice. Just as she was too lost in the deep, hungry kiss to be self-conscious about the new size of her body against him.

Her breasts felt tight and exquisitely tender as she pressed them against his bare skin. She could feel the heat of him even through her top and bra, and she ached to feel his hands, his mouth on them. Was this the result of pregnancy hormones or just the way she always reacted to Andrew's kisses? Whichever the reason, she craved his touch more than the oxygen she gasped in when he lifted his mouth only long enough to change the angle of the kiss.

He was notably aroused against her thigh. It thrilled her that he still reacted to her this way, still wanted her despite her shape or their situation. He slipped a hand between them, beneath her loose top, cupping one taut breast through her bra. His thumb circled lazily, making her gasp into his mouth.

"Maybe—" She paused to clear her throat. "Maybe I'll win that argument after all. Stay with me, Andrew."

"There's nothing I want more than to spend the night in your bed," he said, his voice somewhat deeper and rougher than usual. "But I don't want you to have any regrets."

Would she regret spending another night with him? Or could she see this as one last indulgence just for herself, before she became responsible full-time for a totally dependent child? She wanted him, he wanted her—they were both unattached adults who could use a little stress relief. "No regrets," she promised.

His hand slid downward from her breast to the curve of her belly. "You—uh—I mean, it's okay if we…"

"According to Dr. Power, it's perfectly safe. Even healthy."

His lips quirked into a sexy smile even as his eyes darkened. "Good to know. I'll be careful."

She slid her hand slowly up his chest, skimming very lightly over the scrapes and bruises. "So will I."

Drawing her against him again, he murmured against her lips, "Anything you want."

"You," she whispered between kisses. "I want you."

Wrapping an arm around her shoulders, he turned with her toward the bedroom.

Chapter Seven

Hannah smelled coffee when she woke, reminding her that she hadn't spent the night alone. As if she'd needed that reminder, she thought, stretching slowly in the tangled bedclothes. Her body was pleasantly loose and relaxed, a result of great sex and sound sleep. Perhaps there had been some awkwardness at first, and maybe they'd had to be more careful and restrained than they had during that intense, hot, memorable encounter in Dallas, yet last night Andrew had proved that he was just as skilled at being slow and tender, she thought with a reflective sigh. A long and complicated day lay ahead, but at least she was tackling it after a satisfying and restful night.

She dressed quickly in khaki maternity pants and a summery, floral-printed top in shades of purple and cream. She left her dark hair down to her shoulders,

applied her usual daytime makeup and slid her feet
into leather flip-flops before leaving the bedroom. She
needed to look put-together and collected, which meant
she didn't want to be wearing her nightclothes when she
faced Andrew over the breakfast table.

The mobile home was laid out with the main area—
living room, kitchen and dining room—in the center
and bedrooms with en suite baths at each end. Dressed
in clean jeans and a blue-and-white-striped collared
pullover, evidence that he'd made a quick trip to Steven's place, Andrew sat at the table with a cup of coffee,
frowning down at his phone as he read and answered
emails. She hadn't heard the shower running. Had he
bathed in the guest bath here or at Steven's? Even on a
Saturday morning, he seemed to be inundated with mes-
sages. She thought again of how difficult it must have
been for him to push everything else aside to come here
almost the moment he'd found out about her pregnancy.

He glanced up when she appeared and immediately
put his phone down, giving her a smile that warmed her
blood all over again. His hair was still slightly damp,
and he'd slapped a clean bandage over the cut at his
temple. A purple bruise spread from beneath the bandage almost to his eye. She'd bet that the other bruises
she had discovered on his body during the night had
bloomed as colorfully.

"I made coffee," he said. "Decaf was all I could find
in your cupboards, so I'm assuming you've cut out caf-
feine."

"I have," she said, moving to pour herself a cup.
"Have you had breakfast?"

"Not yet. I thought I'd wait for you. I was going to

make omelets, but I wasn't sure if you have any special dietary requirements."

She grimaced. "I can't handle a heavy breakfast right now. I've been eating fruit and yogurt and wheat toast. I'd be happy to make something for you, though."

He shook his head. "Coffee's good for now."

She carried her cup to the little table, taking the chair across from him. She should probably eat something, but she had no appetite just then. It occurred to her that this was their first real "morning after," because she'd all but kicked him out of her hotel room before dawn the one other night they'd spent together. And while there was an awkwardness to this morning, it felt just a little too right to sit at a breakfast table with Andrew. Right enough that it made a small, hidden part of her heart start to yearn for things she would be wiser to resist.

"I glanced in the spare room a few minutes ago," Andrew commented. "I was surprised to see that with the exception of the twin bed, there's nothing in there."

"I just never got around to furnishing that room, because there was no real reason to do so before." Not to mention that the credit card debts Wade had saddled her with had left her little spare money for furniture, she chose not to add. "Now that I'll be using the room for a nursery, it's probably a good thing I have a bare slate to start with."

"You haven't bought anything for the baby yet?"

"No, not yet. I was waiting until the final trimester to start shopping."

"I'll set up an account for you to use to order what you need online," he said with a nod. "Or would you rather have cash to purchase locally?"

He must have seen the way she immediately tensed.

He spoke quickly before she could. "Sorry, that sounded a little blunt, didn't it? I tend to get into business mode when numbers are involved. I just want you to know, I fully intend to help support this child. No matter what happens between us in the future, you will never have to worry about my being a deadbeat dad."

She had no doubt of that. If anything, she worried more about his being too involved, rather than the opposite—if only because she wasn't sure how she would handle seeing him on a regular basis with her feelings for him so powerful and convoluted.

Because she didn't want to talk about money—or the future—at that moment, she looked toward the stove. "Are you sure I can't get you anything to eat? I have eggs, yogurt, fruit."

He studied her for a moment, then decided to follow her conversational lead, though she supposed he knew as well as she that they were only postponing the inevitable. Again. "I'll have something at the grill later. I want to get started on the investigation."

When it came to that mission, he was focused and determined, she thought with a slight shake of her head. There was no derailing him now.

"To be honest, I think it *was* Chuck," she told him. "But I'm not sure you'll be able to prove it, and I seriously doubt you'll get him to admit it."

Andrew grunted.

"Even though you never met Chuck last year, he's probably heard that you're the P.I. who found the evidence to prosecute Wade. I'm sure he hates you as much as he hates me. Maybe you should stay away from him."

"I'm not afraid of him. But I'm going to make damn sure he's afraid of me by the time I'm done with him. If

I can prove he had anything to do with the sabotage to your home, he's going to join his worthless son in jail."

The fury he'd shown last night was well-banked now, but she saw the anger that still simmered just beneath the civilized surface. She understood how he felt. She would like very much to get her hands on the person who had threatened her daughter, and who had put those bruises on Andrew's face. "So what are you going to do first?"

"I'll ask around, do some research, check a few leads," he said vaguely. "What are your plans for today?"

"I need to update the events calendar at the resort website, post some photos on our social networking sites. We're going to run a special offer to encourage off-season reservations, and I planned to work on that a bit more today."

"You'll be at your desk, then? Plenty of people around there, so you should be okay."

"I'll be fine."

His eyes were dark and somber when they met hers. "You know I have to go back to Dallas tomorrow. I can probably be back here Thursday evening. Friday at the latest."

Looking down into her barely tasted coffee, she nodded. "There's no need for you to rush back. Take care of your responsibilities there. If it will make you feel better, I promise to be extra careful."

"What would make me feel better is if you come with me to Dallas. I started to ask you last night, but we were interrupted by that thump on the wall, and then my fall and, um, everything."

She set down her cup with a thump. "Come with you? Tomorrow?"

He studied her closely. "Yes. Every task you just listed for your job can be done on a computer in my home office. Someone else can sit at the reception desk while you handle the marketing, right? I mean, that's the part of your job you specifically trained for and that you like the best."

She planned to take over the marketing and events scheduling full-time after the baby was born. The family had already discussed hiring someone from outside to run the reception desk full-time so it wouldn't have to divide her time any longer, especially with a baby to care for. Lori was available to man the desk during her summer break, with Mimi there to relieve her, so certainly it would be possible for Hannah to take off for another couple of days. Which didn't mean she was going to do so.

"I don't think it's necessary for me to actually leave the resort. You pointed out yourself that I'll be surrounded by family—probably more than usual now. I'll be safe while you're away."

Andrew shook his head. "It isn't just your safety—though I have to confess that's the most compelling reason I'm asking. You have to admit it's been almost impossible for us to have a long, serious discussion here. Every time we start, we're interrupted. We could talk in Dallas over dinners. Make some plans, some decisions. And maybe I could introduce you to my parents. You'd like my mom. You know she's a senior partner in an ad agency, right? The two of you actually have quite a bit in common."

She swallowed hard. His parents. Her child's other

grandparents. Of course she should meet them, because they would be an important part of her daughter's life—but not yet. Surely she could face that ordeal later.

He must have seen the panic in her expression. His face softened. "Hannah, it's time for us to…"

Someone knocked loudly on her front door, cutting through his words. Andrew sighed. "See what I mean?"

She was already on her feet and moving toward the door, seizing the interruption with relief bordering on sheepish cowardice.

"It's probably Aaron," Andrew said, rising more slowly from the table. "He's meeting me here this morning to get a closer look around the place in daylight."

Rather than Aaron, she found her father standing on her porch, a piece of broken railing in his hand and a frown of concern on his weathered face. "Hannah, what on earth happened here? You didn't fall, did you?"

"No, Dad, I didn't fall. But Andrew did."

He looked both relieved and worried in response to that information. "Is he hurt?"

"I'm fine, Bryan," Andrew said, moving to stand behind her.

Her dad studied Andrew's bruised face, and she wondered if he was asking himself what Andrew was doing there so early. "You'd better come in, Dad. We need to talk to you about what happened."

Shaking his head, her father glared down at the board in his hand as he entered. "I can't figure out how this would have happened. I built that porch and railing myself. I've never seen one just snap like this."

"It didn't exactly snap," Andrew said, motioning him toward the table. "Let me get you some coffee and I'll tell you about it."

If her dad had questions about Andrew's presence there or his apparent comfort in Hannah's kitchen, he was too distracted by last night's events to mention it. It was all Hannah and Andrew could do to talk him out of storming off to find Chuck Cavender after he heard about the deliberate damage to the handrail. Maybe Andrew didn't try very hard to stop him, because he still seemed inclined to confront Chuck himself.

"I never liked that man," Hannah's dad muttered. "I tried to be civil while Hannah and Wade were married, but there's nothing to stop me from whupping his ass now."

Hannah's father was not a violent man; in fact, he was one of the kindest, gentlest men she knew—unless anyone threatened his family. "We don't even know it was Chuck," she reminded him. "Let Andrew and Aaron look into it, okay?"

"I don't want you staying alone. You need to move back into the house with your mom and me until this is settled."

Hannah sighed. Why was everyone so determined not to leave her alone? She really was capable of taking care of herself. "We'll talk about it later, Dad."

"Perhaps it's best if we don't discuss this in front of your grandmother right now," he suggested. "The past few weeks have been a bit too eventful for her."

"She may have already heard," Hannah warned him. "Maggie and Shelby and Aaron and Steven all know about it. They were around when Andrew fell."

"You should have called me," her dad chided.

"There was nothing you could do last night," she replied with a shrug. "And, um, Andrew's been keeping an eye on things here—just as a precaution. An unnecessary precaution, I'm sure."

She wouldn't mention just how close an eye Andrew had kept on her last night, of course.

Her dad nodded toward Andrew. "I appreciate your watching out for her."

Andrew gave Hannah a quick, wry look before replying, "My pleasure."

Her dad went out to look at the porch again, promising to have it repaired that very morning.

"I wonder if he's still going to be so grateful to me when he finds out I'm the father of your child," Andrew murmured when he and Hannah were alone again for those few moments. "Could be *my* butt that will get whupped."

She tucked a strand of hair behind her ear, thinking that she was going to have to find a chance to tell her family the truth very soon. All these secrets and subterfuges, in addition to work, her uncertain future with Andrew and wondering just how crazy her ex-father-in-law had become were starting to fray her nerves. She still wasn't looking forward to the pressure that would be put on Andrew to "do the right thing by her" or on herself to let him, but she'd handle that when it came up.

"I'm going to work," she announced, needing something to do.

"You haven't had breakfast," Andrew reminded her.

"I'm a little queasy this morning. I'll have some crackers at my desk."

He nodded and carried his coffee cup to the sink. "I'll drive you."

"I can—" She sighed when he gave her a look over his shoulder. "Fine. Let's go."

* * *

"So, Shelby has postulated another of her theories," Aaron commented an hour later from the passenger seat of Andrew's car. "I know her family sometimes makes fun of her vivid imagination, but you have to admit she's often right."

"I've always respected Shelby's instincts," Andrew agreed somewhat absently. His attention was divided between his driving, his pleasurable memories of the night before and his concerns about his future with Hannah and the baby. Shelby's latest brainstorm was low on his list of interests at the moment, though he made an effort to keep up his part of the conversation. "Does her new theory have anything to do with who's been harassing Hannah?"

"No, she pretty much agrees with everyone else on that. Thinks it's probably Chuck Cavender. Though her new suspicion does concern Hannah. And you."

Andrew's fingers tightened reflexively on the steering wheel. Aaron had his full attention now. "Does it?"

"Hmm. As in…she's wondering if you and Hannah have seen each other at least once since you left the resort last August."

Andrew would not lie to his twin, but he'd made a promise to Hannah that he wouldn't share their secret just yet. So he remained quiet.

Aaron read that silence perfectly. "Damn, Shelby's right, isn't she?"

Andrew shot his brother a look, taking in his stunned expression before turning his eyes back to the road ahead.

Aaron turned sideways in the passenger seat. "You're

the father of Hannah's baby. You'd have already denied it if you weren't."

"Which direction do I turn at the intersection?"

Impatiently, Aaron consulted the notes in his hand. "Turn right. I assume Hannah has forbidden you to tell? But from what I think I've learned about her, I bet she didn't order you to outright lie in response to a direct question. Are you the father of Hannah's child?"

Aaron was right of course, that Hannah wouldn't expect him to blatantly lie to his brother's direct question. She would never ask that of him.

"Yes." The relief of finally sharing the truth with his twin was immediate. "She's going to tell everyone else soon. In the meantime…"

"I won't give it away," Aaron promised, sounding stunned. "I won't even confirm Shelby's theory to her— well, unless she asks me outright of course."

Andrew shrugged, figuring Shelby would know within ten minutes of their returning to the resort. It would probably be the first thing she asked Aaron upon seeing him again. He sent a silent apology to Hannah, but he'd warned her that the longer they waited the more likely it was that the secret would come out anyway.

"Wow. So you're going to be a father. And I'm an uncle," Aaron marveled. "Mom and Dad are going to freak."

Swallowing hard, Andrew muttered, "Um, yeah. Probably. Let's just say it's been a momentous week for me."

"No kidding. So you and Hannah have been seeing each other since you worked for them last summer? Why didn't you tell anyone?"

"We haven't been seeing each other. It was only the

one night," Andrew admitted. "I hadn't even heard from her since."

He needed to think of a better way to phrase that in the future. He didn't want anyone thinking he and Hannah had indulged in a cheap one-night stand. It had been much more than that—for him at least—though he had yet to come up with an explanation that made sense. Probably because he still didn't know why she'd spent that night with him when she was only going to shoot him down afterward.

"Hey, wait a minute. Am I the one who told you Hannah's pregnant? You really didn't know until I mentioned it on the phone the other day?"

He grimaced. "No, I didn't know."

"Dude."

Andrew nodded glumly.

Aaron rode in silence for a couple minutes, digesting the information, then chuckled drily. "You know what's funny? Just a couple weeks ago, I wished that for once *you'd* do something to scandalize the family and take some attention from my issues for a change."

"Yeah, that's freaking hilarious," Andrew grumbled.

"Sorry. So how do you feel about it? Suddenly finding out you're about to be a dad, I mean."

"Nervous. Pleased. Worried. Proud. A little embarrassed to find myself in this situation at my age. Scared spitless about the responsibility."

"Those all sound like perfectly reasonable reactions," Aaron conceded. "But, um, maybe you should let me do the talking when we get to Cavender's house. You have too much emotionally invested this time to be objective."

Andrew's fingers white-knuckled around the wheel.

"Hannah could have lost the baby," he grated, the words ripping almost painfully from his throat.

Aaron touched his arm, the gesture carrying a wealth of understanding. "I know. And I'm furious about that, too. But it won't help anything if you beat the guy to a pulp before we even have any proof that he's involved."

"It would sure as hell make me feel better." Andrew sighed gustily. "Fine. You do the talking."

Aaron nodded in determination. "He'll lie of course, but maybe we can get a feel for the truth. After that, we'll figure out a way to prove it. And in the meantime, maybe knowing we're on to him will stop him from trying anything else."

"Especially if I promise to beat him to the pulp you mentioned if he ever even looks at Hannah again."

"Uh, yeah, that should probably do it." Aaron suddenly spoke with a bit more care, seeming to choose his words carefully. "So what's going to happen with you and Hannah? You know her grandmother, at the least, is going to be pushing for a wedding. Wouldn't be surprised if Mom drops a few broad hints about that, too."

Andrew tensed again. "We haven't had a chance to talk about the future yet. Hell, we've hardly had a chance to talk at all. Every time we try, we're interrupted."

"It is hard to find privacy at the resort," Aaron agreed.

Andrew slanted his brother a questioning look. "That doesn't bother you?"

Aaron shrugged. "It's just part of the package. I'm not complaining, I like the family. Maybe someday Shelby and I will get a place nearby and commute to work there, but we're good in her trailer for now."

For himself, Andrew couldn't imagine living that way. As fond as he was of the Bell family and as much as he liked their resort, his home was in Dallas. He'd trained from childhood to work in his own family's business, and he thrived there. Yet he had a place of his own, a life outside his job and family, and he needed that, too. He wanted to be with Hannah, fully intended to help her raise their daughter, but even for them he couldn't see himself being happy or fulfilled giving up his career and trying to find something to do with himself here.

Did Hannah feel the same way about her job in the resort, her home surrounded by her family? And if so, where did that leave them in the future?

"This is the place," Aaron said, drawing Andrew from his troubled thoughts. "On the left."

The Cavenders' house was a simple, white-sided ranch-style in a working-class neighborhood. No vehicle was parked in the short driveway, and the garage door was closed. Andrew saw no sign of life around the place, but that didn't mean no one was home, he reminded himself. He stood just behind Aaron on the stoop when Aaron rang the doorbell, braced for a confrontation in which he would be forced to call upon all his self-control. But the bell went unanswered after the third time Aaron pressed the button, and they had to concede the house was probably empty.

"They're gone," someone called out from the almost-identical house next door, drawing the twins' attention in that direction.

An older man in faded jeans, boots and a short-sleeved Western-cut shirt stood by the mailbox at the end of the adjacent driveway, looking their way. "They left for vacation yesterday," he added, his voice raised so they could hear him clearly. "Won't be back for a week. I'm collecting their mail and papers for them."

Andrew frowned, remembering that Hannah had spotted Chuck when they were on the way to the doctor's office yesterday afternoon. "When did they leave?"

"Maybe about five o'clock? Got a late start because Justine had to work yesterday."

"Do you know where they went?" Aaron asked.

The man looked at them narrowly. "Not sure as I should say. Who are you guys anyway?"

"We're acquainted with their son," Aaron replied.

The neighbor looked as though he wanted to spit then—a sentiment Andrew understood too well. "That don't hardly recommend you to me."

"We aren't friends with their son, sir," Andrew explained. "We represent his ex-wife. We're investigating some threats against her."

The man had approached them now, his walk marked with a slight limp, his grizzled face still suspicious. He stopped close enough that they could speak in normally modulated voices, frowning but seemingly relieved to hear they didn't claim friendship with Wade. "I know Chuck blames the ex-wife for everything that went wrong with his boy, though Justine doesn't seem to entirely agree with him. I met the girl only a couple of times, but she seemed nice enough. Too good for Wade, if you ask me."

Andrew nodded in concurrence.

The old man scratched his stubbly chin. "Wouldn't think Chuck would go so far as to make threats against her, though. He can be surly, but he's not completely stupid."

"We're simply looking into all possibilities," Aaron said.

The older man nodded and reached a decision, blurting out, "Chuck and Justine have gone to visit Chuck's mama in Beaumont. Her last name is Cavender, too, but can't remember her first name. Wade's ex probably knows, so if you're working for her, you can ask her. No need for you to mention how you found out where they are if you talk to Chuck of course."

Andrew nodded. "No, sir. We won't involve you. Thank you for the information."

"Well, that was a waste of time," Aaron said when they were in the car again.

"Maybe not entirely. Maybe the old man will tell Chuck someone's looking into him, which could serve as a warning in the future. And we'll definitely follow up. In the meantime, you need to get those closed-circuit cameras installed ASAP."

Bryan had agreed that one of the cameras would record the area around the trailers, while others would be aimed at the houses, at the main building, the motel parking lot and a couple of places in the campgrounds for a total of six units. Signs would be posted that the resort was monitored by security cameras.

"Bryan and I are going to start on that this afternoon," Aaron agreed. "Tomorrow we'll reinforce the barrier at the end of the old road. We're thinking concrete blocks."

They had been somewhat surprised to discover that the chain was still in place and the road looked undisturbed. They'd agreed that either Cavender had somehow come in through the gate or had walked in on the old road, a long trek over rough ground, but certainly doable. He'd have gone to a great deal of trouble just to sabotage Hannah's porch, but hatred and bitterness could lead to extreme acts, as Andrew had seen on more than one occasion in his career.

"So, you know my schedule for today. What are you going to do the rest of the day?" Aaron asked when Andrew parked again in Steven's driveway.

"I have some work I can do from here. And I promised C.J. I'd run a standard background check on Lori's boyfriend. If you and Bryan need me to help with the camera installation, give me a call."

Aaron chuckled. "This family does have a way of keeping you busy, huh?"

"I volunteered for the latest assignments. I'm not expecting to find much about the boyfriend, though. Not without a full surveillance operation."

"I don't even want to think about how Lori would react to that," Aaron said with an exaggerated shudder.

Andrew frowned. "Lori."

"Yeah, what about her?"

Suddenly remembering the tense exchange he'd interrupted earlier, Andrew said, "She and Hannah were quarreling earlier today. I didn't catch it all, but I think it had something to do with Lori's boyfriend. You don't think—"

"That Lori would do anything to hurt Hannah?" Aaron asked incredulously. "You can't mean that. I've known her only a couple of weeks and I still don't believe it."

Andrew considered it a few moments, then shook his head. "No, I don't know Lori very well either, but I can't accept that. The boyfriend, though—if he thinks Hannah is working against him with the family, maybe..."

"Still iffy. Hannah only found out about Lori and Zach when she got back from Shreveport. As far as I know, she's done nothing to interfere with them, other than maybe offering some advice Lori didn't accept."

"You're right," Andrew said with a shrug. "Just considering all the angles."

"You always do."

"I try." Andrew climbed out of the car and pushed a hand through his hair. "Doesn't mean I always get it right."

He'd been trying to consider all the angles in his convoluted relationship with Hannah, for example. And he couldn't begin to predict what would ultimately happen between them. Or even tomorrow, for that matter. All he knew was that he was far from ready to say goodbye to her.

The three men Hannah had secretly dubbed "the stooges" checked out Saturday afternoon. Nathan Burns, the one who'd made the reservations, handled the key exchange, while his buddies picked up sodas and snacks from the store for their drive home. He assured her that their stay had been quite satisfactory, that they'd caught some fish, hiked nearby trails and engaged in some quality buddy-bonding time. "All around great time," he concluded.

Handing him his receipt, she smiled. "I'm glad you had fun. We hope you'll come back and visit us again in the future."

"I'm sure we will." Touching the brim of his ball cap in an old-fashioned gesture, he turned to join his friends, who waited for him at the big glass exit doors. Hannah hid a smile when the one she'd dubbed "Skinny

Romeo" glanced her way, flushed, then turned to leave, obviously still embarrassed that he'd hit on her so clumsily upon arrival and had been so firmly shot down. She'd seen him once or twice since, and wasn't sure he'd been sober the whole time. Although he hadn't actually caused any trouble, that was one guest she'd just as soon not see again anytime soon.

She glanced toward the grill, noting that business was still heavy with late lunchers, even though it was almost 2:00 p.m. She'd bet her aunt Sarah would appreciate the brief slowdown they'd probably see after the weekend, though business would get crazy again as the Independence Day weekend approached. From her desk, she could see one corner of the inside of the diner. Customers mingled, chatted, ate, laughed. At a far table, Patricia Gibson ate alone as always, her attention focused on her food, her hunched posture discouraging any friendly overtures. Perhaps she'd thought she'd avoid a crowd by dining later, but Hannah could have told her that on a summer Saturday, the place was always hopping.

Maybe the stooges had enjoyed their stay, but she saw no evidence that Patricia was having a good time. She wondered why the woman even stayed when her entire schedule seemed to be split between staying in her room and occasionally eating a meal here. How much longer would she stay? Hannah felt as though she should offer to do something to make the visit more pleasant, but she couldn't think of anything else to say or do. Patricia had been fairly clear that she wanted to be left alone.

A shadow fell over her desk and she looked around with a professional smile that quavered just a bit when she saw Andrew standing there, looking delectable as always despite his bandage and bruises. Memories of the night before slammed through her, making her have to swallow before attempting to greet him breezily. "Hi."

He leaned comfortably against the end of the reception desk. "Hi, how's it going?"

"It's been busy. Between the phone and guests, I haven't been able to get to the marketing work I wanted to do today."

Andrew shook his head. "You're trying to do too much."

"I agree," she said wryly. "I think it's time we hire a couple more people for office work. We thought we'd hold off a couple months until Lori goes back to school, but that's not working out. I'm going to run a help wanted ad next week."

"But you could take off next week if you decide to accompany me to Dallas?"

"I suppose I could," she reluctantly conceded. "But I—"

"Don't decide just yet," he cut in. "Think about it some more, okay?"

She nodded, relieved to have a respite. "Did you talk to Chuck?"

"He's out of town. Left last night, won't be back for a week. Visiting his mother, reportedly."

"In Beaumont?"

He nodded. "That's what I was told. Do you know her name and address so I can check that?"

"I have it in my files. She lives in an assisted living facility. Wade was never particularly interested in visiting his grandmother, but I met her a couple of times. She's a little vague."

He nodded. "I'll look into it."

"Do you think leaving town rules Chuck out or makes it even more likely that he broke my porch, then ran?"

"Could be either. But at least he's not around to bother you for a few days, assuming he really is in Beaumont."

"Then there's no need for me to leave. I'd be fine staying here," she pointed out.

Andrew frowned. "You're still assuming Chuck was behind the incidents. I haven't proven that. I'm not going to be completely comfortable leaving you unprotected until I know for certain."

She resisted an impulse to roll her eyes. "I'm hardly unprotected. My sister and cousins have stopped by every ten minutes or so today to check on me."

"I'd still rather have you with me," he said, his voice dropping to an intimate level that made a little shiver course down her spine.

"I'll, um, I'll think about it," she told him again.

He nodded and straightened from the desk. "I assume you've already eaten lunch?"

"Yes, I had a sandwich earlier."

"Maybe I'll just get a cup of soup to hold me until dinner." He glanced toward the diner. "Your aunt makes good soup."

Following his glance, she saw Patricia leaving the diner, directing a hooded glance toward Hannah and Andrew on her way out. Hannah offered a little wave, which Patricia returned with a glum nod.

"She's still here?" Andrew seemed surprised. "I haven't seen her since I moved out of the motel."

"Still here. I'm not sure how much longer she's staying."

"Wonder what her story is."

Hearing the thoughtful curiosity in his tone, Hannah laughed softly and shook her head. "You can't run checks on everyone in the resort, Andrew. You're already looking into Chuck and Zach. Have you found out anything about Zach, by the way?"

"That's what I've been doing since I got back from Cavender's place. Zach's juvenile records are sealed and he's kept his nose clean for at least the past couple of years. His band has a few upcoming gigs, and he works part-time giving guitar lessons. He spends a lot of time in bars and clubs, but considering his career aspirations, that's to be expected."

Hannah frowned. "Hardly the most secure career he could pursue. Not to mention the lifestyle that goes along with it—constant travel, uncertain income, groupies, drugs…I'd hate to see Lori get wrapped up in all that."

Andrew chuckled. "Now who's being overprotective? Not to mention that you're stereotyping every young guy who ever played in a band. I have a couple of cousins who went through the band stage, and they've all turned out okay. Your cousin's just going through the typical rebellion stage, I wouldn't worry about it too much."

"You're probably right," Hannah conceded sheepishly. "I guess it comes from being the oldest. I tend to think I have to look after the others."

"My cousin Jason would identify with that," Andrew said with a chuckle.

"Is he an eldest cousin, too?"

"Well, technically, he's the second of the fifteen Walker cousins, but there's a sixteen-year gap between him and my oldest cousin, Brynn. He's always seemed like the first of our generation, while Brynn seems more comfortable with our parents."

Her baby was going to have a lot of relatives, Hannah thought a few minutes later, after Andrew left to eat. She had to occasionally remind herself that the child was as much a Walker as she was a Bell. Just as her parents were going to have to get used to the idea of sharing their grandchild with another set of grandparents. She sighed, telling herself that the sooner she and Andrew broke the news, the sooner everyone could start adjusting. It seemed clear that tonight at dinner would be the natural time, which meant she would warn Andrew to be prepared for the resulting fallout. She had only a few hours to brace herself and decide exactly what she wanted to say.

Chapter Eight

Andrew just happened to be hanging around when Hannah was ready to go back to her place before the planned dinner with her parents. Resisting an impulse to sigh, she climbed into a golf cart with him and allowed him to drive her the half mile home, though she had planned to walk for the exercise. It just seemed easier not to argue. This time.

He insisted on checking her steps and newly constructed railing before she climbed the stairs to her front door. Only when he'd confirmed that everything was solid did he move aside to allow her to enter.

"Thank you," she said, her sarcasm either sailing over his head or simply going unacknowledged as he followed her in.

"Are you kidding?" she murmured when he then made a show of checking all the windows and the back door for signs of entrance. "Don't you think you're carrying this a little too far?"

"Not where your safety is concerned," he replied, unperturbed by her tone. "Everything looks good."

"Of course it does." Shaking her head, she motioned toward the kitchen. "There's iced tea in the fridge if you want a glass. I want to freshen up before we head to Mom and Dad's house. Or, of course, you could meet me there later."

"I'll have some tea," he said, not at all to her surprise. He wasn't leaving her alone even for the half hour remaining before they were expected to join her family for dinner. She was going to have to discuss this with him of course. She would be smothered if she couldn't have even a few minutes to herself, and she needed to convince him that she was perfectly capable of using caution on her own behalf. It was just one of the many things they were going to talk about after she washed her face, freshened her makeup and brushed her hair— all an excuse to give her a few minutes alone to compose her arguments.

He sat on the couch when she returned, a half-filled glass of tea on the coffee table, his ever-present phone in his hand. More work emails, she suspected. His responsibilities in Dallas had to be weighing on his mind as much as his concerns here.

She sat on the other end of the couch, half turned to face him. "Andrew—"

He set his phone aside. "You want me to back off. I'm trying."

He had a real knack for knowing exactly what she was about to say. Still, she said, "You can't be my full-time bodyguard."

"I know," he conceded with visible reluctance. He reached out to cover her hand on her knee with his. "I just want to take care of you."

Something inside her melted in response to his words and the gentle tone in which he'd said them, but she made herself stay strong. "You know, since I found the backbone to divorce Wade a year and a half ago, I've gotten into the habit of taking care of myself. I like it."

"I know that, too. And I have to admit, it makes me wonder if there's a place for me in the life you've made for yourself."

She moistened her lips, trying to decide what he meant. Was he saying he wanted a place in her life? Permanently?

The baby gave a particularly vigorous kick to her rib cage, probably because she was twisted on the couch, and she shifted into a more comfortable position, her free hand going automatically to her side. Andrew followed that movement with his eyes. "Is she kicking?"

"Yes. Do you want to feel her?" After their lovemaking last night, he had been fascinated by the hard little lumps and bumps beneath her skin, the rolling, kicking movements of their child inside her. Hannah had fallen asleep very quickly, but she wondered how long Andrew had lain awake, thinking about the future, visualizing the daughter he would be meeting in a few months.

"Of course," he said, pressing his palm to her side, just where the baby's foot was performing a little tap dance. "Wow, she's really getting her exercise, isn't she?"

"Getting stronger every day."

He slowly moved his hand away, as though he would

have liked to leave it there longer. "I haven't even thought to ask if you have a name for her yet."

"Not really. After all, we just found out yesterday that she's a girl." It made her head spin a bit to realize how much had happened in the past few days. It was no wonder she hadn't found time to make lists of potential names. "Um, do you have any favorite girls' names?"

Looking a little dazed, he shook his head. "I haven't thought about it yet, either. I mean, choosing a name for our kid makes it all pretty real, doesn't it?"

It had been real for Hannah for several months now, but Andrew still had a way to go to catch up. "Yes."

"She'll probably have dark hair, because you and I both inherited our mothers' dark coloring. My dad's hair is lighter, and his eyes are light blue. So our daughter's eyes could be any color, but I hope she gets your jade-green. You have beautiful eyes."

From Andrew, that was almost a poetic speech. It made her cheeks warm in instinctive pleasure. "She may well have your brown eyes, because I believe brown is dominant, but we'll see."

"Whichever, she'll still be beautiful."

"Yes." Hannah had no doubt that their daughter would be beautiful to them. She already loved this baby so much her heart ached with it. She suspected Andrew was quickly feeling the same way. Family was as important to him as to her, and he made no secret of his affection for them.

As for their feelings for each other...

She loved him, she thought with a hard swallow. She had loved him almost from the beginning. He'd come into her life at a time of turmoil, bringing with him sanity, certainty and reassurance. He'd listened to her, respected her, comforted her and deferred to her—all things she and her battered ego had needed at that time. She'd fallen for his compassion, his competence, his quiet humor, his undeniable physical appeal. The whole package. She'd loved him when she'd invited him into her bed in Dallas, even though she'd been convinced then it wouldn't last. Now she knew she would love him the rest of her life.

Maybe he was trying to convince himself he loved her, too. But despite her own certainty, how could she trust his feelings to last, considering the current circumstances? He wouldn't even be here with her now if it were not for her unexpected pregnancy. Yes, she had been the one to ask him not to contact her after that night in December, but she'd had good reasons then, and still thought her decision had been valid. Maybe just as valid now.

"Hannah—"

"Claire," she blurted in a sudden panic at what he might say. "I've always liked the name Claire. Do you like it?"

He blinked, then nodded. "I like it."

"My mother's middle name is Elizabeth. I think Claire Elizabeth is a pretty name, don't you?"

"Very nice."

Claire Elizabeth…Bell? Walker? Bell-Walker? She suspected that question nagged at Andrew just as it did at her. He didn't have to tell her which he preferred. She knew he wanted his child to carry his name. But he would probably agree to whatever she ultimately decided, as long as he had an active role in the child's life.

"Have you given any more thought to going with me to Dallas tomorrow?"

She tucked her hair behind her left ear. "I'm still thinking about it."

"You haven't entirely ruled it out?"

"No," she admitted. She wasn't afraid to stay here, but maybe she should be with him when he told his parents about the baby. It would only be fair, because she planned to tell hers with him there tonight.

It would be natural for his parents to worry about what he'd gotten himself into, maybe even to question the character of the woman who was carrying his baby. As far as she knew, Andrew wasn't one of the super-wealthy, but from what she'd gleaned about them, his family lived quite comfortably. They owned businesses and had a reputation to consider. Putting herself in their shoes, she could see how they would be concerned if he simply told them out of the blue that he was having a child with a woman they'd never met. She supposed she owed it to him as a simple courtesy to meet and reassure them, especially because Andrew was going out of his way to accommodate her on so many counts.

"I'll talk to the family, see if there would be any problem with my taking another week off," she conceded. "I still haven't decided, but maybe."

The flare of satisfaction in his eyes suggested he was confident she would be leaving with him tomorrow. "Good."

She started to warn him again not to be so certain, but decided to let it go. It was true that she hadn't ruled it out, so maybe she would go. Actually, maybe she'd be glad to get away for a few days after tonight.

"I've decided we should tell my family at dinner," she said, knowing there was no need to be more specific. "You're right, the longer I wait, the more likely it is they'll find out anyway. They deserve to hear the truth from me."

Andrew cleared his throat. "I think you should know that Aaron already knows. I didn't tell him," he added quickly. "Shelby figured it out and when Aaron asked me outright if it was true, I couldn't lie to him."

She couldn't be mad at him of course. "Maggie knows, too," she confessed. "For the same reason—she made an educated guess."

Had any other members of her family reached the same conclusion? Her parents? Her aunt or uncle? She doubted that Mimi had, because her grandmother would never be able to keep quiet about it.

"Then it's definitely time you tell your parents," Andrew said. "Your dad's going to give me enough evil-eye looks as it is."

"Dad won't blame you."

"Dads always blame the guy," he retorted. "Just wait a few years and see how I react to any guy who comes sniffing around our daughter."

She bit her lower lip, trying to imagine what it would be like to share a teenage daughter with Andrew.

He cleared his throat, drawing her thoughts back to the present. "How, um, how do you think your family is going to react? Really?"

She'd been trying to predict that since she'd first realized in utter shock that she was pregnant. She'd known from the beginning that eventually she would have to tell them about that night in Dallas—after she'd told Andrew of course. She still didn't know exactly how they would feel about it.

"I think they'll be fine with it," she answered him

cautiously. "Everyone likes you. Maggie was certainly pleased when I confirmed her guess."

"Are you prepared for the questions? About how we got together, I mean."

Her cheeks warmed. "To an extent. They don't need too many details of course."

A quick flare of heat in his eyes made her suspect he was remembering a few of those details himself, but he moved on. "You know your grandparents—and maybe your parents, too—will ask if we plan to marry."

She winced. He had just stated the very reason she'd been so resistant to telling her family. "Yes, probably. Especially Mimi."

"Yeah, she was already trying to push us that way. She'll be even more determined now."

Hannah lifted her chin. "We'll just have to tell her to butt out. I'll try to be gentle about it, but if she persists, I'll have to get firm with her."

"And that's all the answer you plan to give them?" He watched her face closely as he asked, making her wonder just where this was leading.

"I'll make a general statement that we haven't yet worked out the details, but that both of us want you to be an important part of our child's life," she said. "We still have so much to discuss, but the family needs to back off while we make our decisions."

"Just so you know, I think marriage is one of the options we should consider."

She felt her jaw start to drop, and quickly snapped it shut again. Surely he didn't consider that a proposal. If so, it had to be the least romantic attempt ever! Not that she wanted him to go on one knee or anything, she quickly assured herself. More likely, he was just outlining all the options, feasible or not, in that ultraorganized and compulsively thorough manner of his.

She abruptly rose from the couch, having looked ahead just about all she could for the moment. "Maybe we should head on over. I'll see if there's anything I can do to give Mom a hand with dinner."

He stood, sliding his phone into his pocket. She thought she saw him square his shoulders before he said, "Okay, I'm ready. Let's get this over with."

Even though they were a few minutes early, the rest of the family—with the exception of Lori—had already gathered at the home of Hannah's parents. Andrew noted that his entrance with Hannah was greeted in various ways—beaming approval from her grandmother, distracted welcome from her parents, barely veiled excitement from the younger members of the family who were in on the secret. A big brisket had been in the smoker all day to be served with roasted vegetables and yeast rolls. A carnivorous family, this, but then, most of his were, too. While he was generally just as happy with veggies, he had to admit the Texas mesquite-smoked meat smelled delicious.

Like the other two houses in the compound, this one had an open floor plan with bedrooms set off down a hallway on one side and few walls in the common living area. Kitchen, dining and living areas flowed together so that visiting was easier. A large-screen TV hung above a fireplace in one cozy corner formed by a sectional sofa and comfortable chairs; a game table and bookcases filled another corner. Framed photographs covered nearly every surface, mostly of Hannah and Maggie in various stages of growing up, but also quite a few of the rest of the extended family. There was plenty of seating for eating around a table with eight chairs and a quartz-topped bar with four tall stools with padded leather backrests. Because there were exactly twelve for dinner, Aaron, Shelby, Steven and Maggie claimed the barstools, leaving the table for everyone else.

"Is Lori not joining us?" Maggie asked as she helped set out silverware. "She and I had talked about taking a trail ride tomorrow. We haven't done that in forever."

"I haven't heard from her," Sarah complained. "She left this morning without a word to anyone. Your dad and I didn't even see her leave. We were still getting ready for the day. Heaven only knows when she'll be home."

"I know one thing for certain," C.J. said with a scowl, "she and I are going to be having a talk when she finally gets home. This running around at all hours, neglecting her responsibilities at home and work, not even giving us the courtesy of telling us when she's going to be home has got to stop. We've been too lenient with her. We never would have let Steven or Shelby get away with this behavior—not that either of them were ever so inconsiderate."

"Dad, Lori is twenty years old," Shelby pointed out. "You aren't really putting her on a curfew, are you? Not unless you want her to move out."

"We don't want her to move out," Sarah insisted with a hard look at her husband. "We'd just like to know when to expect her so we know when we should worry. That doesn't seem like too much to ask."

"It's not, Mom," Steven agreed from the bar. "Lori's being a brat. I blame that Webber jerk. Bad influence."

Shelby groaned. "Let's not rehash this again. Where were you planning to trail ride, Maggie?"

Maggie took her seat at the bar next to her cousin while the others, seated at the table, began to pass dishes family style. "Rough Rock Stables. You want to go even if Lori doesn't decide to join us?"

"Sure. Aaron's going to be busy all day tomorrow anyway, installing the security barriers with your dad."

Bryan nodded, then glanced at Aaron. "You still want to do that tomorrow, right? I mean, you can take off and go riding with the girls if you want."

"No, that's okay. I'd rather get the security measures in place," Aaron assured him.

Spearing a slice of brisket, Mimi asked, "Do you ride, Aaron?"

Andrew and Aaron shared an amused glance.

"Yes," Aaron said for them both. "We ride. There's really not a lot of choice in our family."

"Your folks own horses?" Pop asked, scooping potatoes onto his plate.

Seated across the table from Pop, Andrew explained. "Our uncle owns a ranch outside of Dallas. He raises horses, a few heads of cattle and boys."

"Boys?" Linda inquired with a quizzical smile.

"The ranch is a home for at-risk foster boys. Has been for years. Our uncle and aunt take them in, give them affection, attention, discipline, education, therapy if necessary. Most of them turn their lives around there, going on to college and/or successful careers afterward, though there have been a very few they just couldn't get through to, who didn't turn out so well. There was a big reunion at the ranch a few years ago with quite a few of the guys who spent time there, and most of them still consider our uncle Jared a surrogate father."

"Well, isn't that nice," Mimi marveled. "Your family really likes children, don't they, Andrew?"

"You could say that," he agreed, carefully avoiding Hannah's gaze. "Our dad is one of seven siblings, all of whom had kids of their own."

He wasn't sure if Aaron had told them about their dad's unconventional background: Ryan Walker and his twin brother, Joe, had been separated from their brothers and sisters as children when their parents died. It had taken them some twenty-five years to find each other again, with the exception of one brother who'd died as a teenager, leaving a pregnant girlfriend as his only known survivor. The Walkers valued family because they all knew what it was like to be separated from each other, and had learned not to take their loved ones for granted afterward. They'd raised their children with that same pro-family ethic.

He'd mishandled that brief conversation with Hannah before dinner. He'd been mentally kicking himself ever since for his awkward broaching of the possibility of marriage. He knew how skittish Hannah was about the subject, especially after overhearing part of her conversation with her sister earlier that week. Rather than just blurting it out as a possibility, he should have made more of an effort to convince her of what a practical, reasonable solution it could be to their situation.

Yes, there were other options, and they should certainly consider them all, but marriage did seem like one of the more logical actions they could take, especially because her job here could rather easily convert to a telecommuting position. To be honest, the more he thought about it, the more he liked the idea of having Hannah and their daughter with him all the time. He would just have to find a way to discuss it with her without having her bolt in panic because of her previous marriage's bitter end.

"I think it's wonderful that your aunt and uncle take in children," Mimi continued with all the subtlety of a freight train. "It just goes to show that it takes more than biology to make a family. Plenty of men adopt children and grow to love them as their own."

"Stop it, Mom," Bryan warned in a grumble, his graying brows drawing into a frown.

The older woman widened her eyes in exaggerated bewilderment. "I don't know what you mean."

"Yes, you do. Eat your dinner."

She sighed gustily and sliced into her meat. Andrew focused intently on his own plate, ignoring the snort of muffled laughter that might have come from his twin.

Ever the gracious hostess, Linda immediately launched into a conversation about an interesting article she'd read online, drawing several others into a discussion with her. Shelby and Maggie continued to plan their riding outing, while Aaron and Steven talked baseball stats. Andrew noted that Hannah was rather subdued as she ate, probably mentally composing the announcement she planned to make after the meal. He had to confess he was having trouble making airy small talk himself.

Shelby gave a sudden gasp, drawing everyone's eyes to her in curiosity. Andrew saw that she was staring down at the screen of her phone, which must have been on vibrate-only mode because he hadn't heard a sound from it. Her face had gone pale, he noted in concern.

"Shelby?" Aaron reached out to touch her arm. "Is something wrong?"

She looked toward her parents with hesitation, looking as though she almost dreaded her next words. "Lori sent me a text. She wants me to tell you that she isn't coming back tonight."

C.J. scowled. "I guess she told you she's staying with 'friends'?"

"No, Dad." Shelby swallowed visibly before saying, "Lori and Zach have eloped. They were married this afternoon."

General chaos erupted after Shelby's shocking announcement. The mostly finished meal forgotten, everyone rose, milling around the room as if trying to decide what they should do in response to this unexpected announcement. Shelby tried texting questions to her sister but received no response.

"That just can't be true," Sarah insisted somewhat frantically. "How could she just elope?"

"You said you didn't see her leave this morning," Andrew said, going immediately into work mode. "So you don't know if she took any of her things?"

"No," Sarah admitted.

"I can go check," Shelby volunteered, looking eager to have something specific to do. "I'll be right back."

Offering to accompany her, Maggie was right behind Shelby as she dashed out the door.

His expression grim, C.J. comforted his tearful wife while Sarah tended to Mimi, who'd gone uncharacteristically quiet with shock, and Bryan hovered near Pop, both looking worried about the impulsive youngest member of the family. Aaron moved closer to Andrew

"Should we try to do something?" he asked. "We could probably track her down."

"And then what?" Andrew asked with a slight shrug. He understood why Aaron felt compelled to make the suggestion, but they had to be reasonable. "Lori's twenty and Webber's twenty-one. That's a legal age to marry in every state. All they had to do was drive to Arkansas, where there's no waiting period, and find a justice of the peace. It's probable they had this planned ahead so they knew exactly what to do."

"She took bags," Shelby reported upon her return with Maggie. "Quite a few of her clothes and shoes are missing, along with toiletries and a few other things I noticed with a quick look around her room."

"So she really did it," Sarah said, sinking slowly into a chair. "She's run off and gotten married."

"To a barely employed musician with a juvenile record," C.J. muttered angrily. "And she's got another year of college to go. Does anyone believe she'll finish now?"

Steven rose to balance on his crutches. "Okay, look, I know you're disappointed, but this isn't the end of the world. Lori's an adult, and she's going to have to make her own decisions. If this marriage works out, that's great for her. If not, well, she'll handle that, too."

Andrew noted that Hannah nodded solemnly. "It won't do any good to yell at her now," she assured them. "She'll just avoid coming around with him. Even if she suspects she made a mistake, she'll need to try to make it work for a while just because she'll have a hard time admitting she should have listened to her parents' advice. My advice would be to try to get to know him, let Lori know you're here for her if you need her—and keep Zach away from the resort finances, just in case," she added with a hint of bitterness.

"No question about that," C.J. muttered. He didn't respond to the rest of her advice, but Andrew figured he'd heard it all and would consider it.

Perhaps needing to return to a semblance of normalcy, Linda began to clear the table. After a moment, the others pitched in to help. Several had tried to contact Lori, but their calls were not being answered for now.

A few minutes later, Hannah moved to Andrew's side in the main living room. He'd been standing in front of a large front window that looked out into the clear summer evening, the view of the resort lights and the distant glimmer of the lake unimpeded by the open drapes.

"What do you see out there?" she asked.

He glanced down at her with a faint smile. "Peace."

Tucking a strand of hair behind her ear, she chuckled softly. "As opposed to in here?"

Half turning away from the window, he glanced toward her family, who mingled through the kitchen and living room conducting low-voiced conversations, probably fretting about Lori. "They seem to have calmed down for the moment."

Hannah sighed. "Yeah, and I'm about to stir them up again."

He felt his left eyebrow rise. "You're still going to tell them tonight? After all this?"

"You're still leaving tomorrow, aren't you?"

"I'm afraid so. I really have to."

"Then we should tell them tonight, so you can prepare your own parents."

"I'm still hoping you'll go with me tomorrow for that."

She shook her head, and her expression was hard to read. "I was considering it, but now I really can't. Without Lori here to work and because we haven't hired extra help yet, I'm going to be needed here."

He told himself he understood. Tried to convince himself he wasn't terribly disappointed. He would be back, he assured himself. Soon.

"And it's not as if this is going to be a hugely dramatic announcement," she continued in a low voice when he remained silent. "I mean, they already know I'm pregnant. They've surely figured out how I got that way. All I'll be doing is filling in a name. I expect they'll approve of the baby's parentage."

He wasn't so sure, nor did he know if she was as prepared as she thought for the pressure that would be put on them after she'd filled in the name, as she'd termed it. But she was probably right that the family wouldn't react as radically as they had to Lori's elopement. He would not be entirely surprised if other members of the family had already figured it out for themselves.

He took her hand and gave it a light squeeze. No matter how confident she tried to sound, he could see the nerves in her eyes. He was a little nervous himself actually. About what her family would say, and about how Hannah would deflect questions about their future intentions. As badly as he'd mishandled the mention of a possible marriage, he had been unable to sufficiently gauge her reaction. It had seemed that her first reaction had been immediate rejection—but had that been because of the awkward way he'd brought up the subject, or because she was completely opposed to the idea?

"I'll back you up on whatever you want to tell them

tonight," he assured her. "But I still want a chance soon to have a long talk just between us."

He thought he saw her swallow as she nodded. "I know."

Still holding her hand, he began to turn with her toward the center of the room.

He heard the loud crash at the same time the window shattered inward behind him. He felt several sharp tingles on his cheek, the back of his neck and his left arm beneath the short sleeve of his shirt. Something heavy slammed to the floor at his feet amid the rain of glass. Without taking time to examine it, he threw himself at Hannah, wrapping himself around her and pushing her away from the object, bracing himself for a possible blast.

Chapter Nine

Her face almost smothered in Andrew's chest, Hannah heard the shocked gasps and cries from around the room. Almost as if from a distance, she felt the sting of myriad cuts on her face, neck and arms, but there was no real pain. She was aware of someone dashing past her, throwing open the front door and bolting outside. Aaron? Followed by C.J., she realized, lifting her head in time to see her uncle disappear outside.

Loosening his grip on her, Andrew looked around cautiously. "A rock," he said in disgust. "It's a big damn rock."

Shakily, she drew away from him, staring in confusion at the grapefruit-size rock sitting on her mother's floor, surrounded by broken glass. "What did you think it was?"

"A grenade. A Molotov cocktail," he admitted grimly. "I didn't take time to pick it up and study it."

No, he hadn't taken that time, she realized in a daze. Instead, he'd put himself between her and the object, covering her with as much of his own body as possible, instinctively protecting her and their child. If she hadn't already been hopelessly in love with him, she'd surely have tumbled then.

"Hannah? Baby, are you all right?" Her father hovered beside her, patting her shoulder, brushing a shard of glass from her hair.

"I'm fine, Dad."

"You're bleeding," her mother fretted from her other side, touching her face. Her fingers came away smeared with red.

Hannah lifted her own hand tentatively, deciding the cuts were superficial. Andrew's lightning-fast reaction might well have prevented her from being sliced by flying glass. She looked at him, seeing minor cuts scattered beneath the bandage from yesterday. None of them appeared deep, to her great relief.

She looked down at the rock and the larger shards of broken glass. Had she and Andrew not been walking away from the window, had they still been standing there in conversation, they could both have been badly injured. As it was, the large rock had missed them both by scant inches, and the larger pieces of glass had fallen just behind them.

"Who could have done this?" Mimi asked plaintively, drawing Hannah's attention in that direction. She saw that her shaken grandmother had been urged into a seat and was being tended to by Sarah and Shelby, while Steven and Maggie stood on either side of their grandfather, who looked more angry than distressed.

"You're okay?" Andrew asked her intently.

Flanked by her parents, she nodded, knowing what he wanted to do. "Go with your brother, but be careful."

He was out the door almost before she finished speaking.

Maggie rushed to get a broom and dustpan to start cleaning up glass. Steven insisted on taking photos with his phone first, and warned Maggie not to touch the rock with her bare hands. "Fingerprints," he explained. "By the way, did anyone notify the police about this?"

Saying he would take care of that, Hannah's dad moved to a phone, while Steven examined the window damage. "We can tape a tarp over this tonight and replace the glass tomorrow," he said. "You'll have to notify your insurance agent of course, if you make a claim for it."

Hannah's mom insisted that Hannah should sit down. She rushed to get a damp washcloth to clean up the thankfully minor cuts Hannah had suffered.

"I really don't understand what's going on around here lately," Mimi bemoaned, wringing her hands. "Shelby was kidnapped, Lori's run off to get married and now someone does this. Has the whole world just gone crazy?"

"Sometimes it seems like it, Mimi," Shelby said, her expression a bit worried as she watched the door for the men to return. "But everyone's okay. We'll face whatever it is together, just like we always do."

Mimi sighed wistfully. "But still, Lori's left, and Steven's leaving soon. Things are changing."

"Things always change in a family, Mimi," Hannah's mother replied, looking meaningfully toward Hannah and the soon-to-be next generation as she approached with the washcloth. "As Shelby said, we'll handle it together. Those who leave will always come back, even if only to visit. And whoever did this will be caught and punished. Everything will be fine."

Hannah figured her mother was trying to reassure herself as well as her mother-in-law. Like everyone else, her mom was still shaken, but staying busy and positive was her way of dealing with it.

The front door opened, and everyone turned quickly to look that way. C.J. entered first, his expression somber but satisfied. Andrew and Aaron entered with someone else gripped between them.

Hannah gasped. "Patricia?"

The habitually morose motel guest shot her a glare of such intense hatred that Hannah instinctively recoiled. What had she done to this woman except try to be a gracious host? Sitting beside her on the couch, her mom gripped her hand in support.

"Caught her running through the woods," Aaron said. Hannah wondered if he'd gotten the scratch on his cheek from a low-hanging tree branch or if Patricia had fought him. "She denies throwing the rock, but it's pretty obvious, considering."

"No one touched the rock, right?" Andrew asked, nodding toward where it still lay.

"No," Steven said, looking pleased with himself for seeing to that.

"Then I think we can prove quite definitively whether she threw the rock. Note that she's not wearing gloves."

Patricia seemed to struggle for a moment between continuing her denials and defiantly claiming her action. She settled on the latter, almost spitting at Hannah, "I wish it had hit you. If you hadn't moved when you did, it would have."

On her feet now, Hannah stared at the other woman in bafflement. "Why? What on earth did I do to you?"

"You took him from me!" she shrieked. "You all did. And I hate you all. I wish that rock had been a bottle full of burning gasoline."

Hannah looked at her mother, her sister, her cousins, trying to see if anyone understood what this woman was ranting about. "Took who from you?"

"Wade! You took Wade!" Patricia was weeping openly now.

Hannah felt her knees give way. She sank to the couch again in shock, realizing she'd been very slow in catching on. "You were one of Wade's women," she said dully.

That, of course, only set Patricia off more. She babbled almost incoherently about how she'd been the only woman Wade had truly loved, how he was now so bitter and unhappy that he wouldn't answer her letters or accept her calls or visits to him in prison, how the stress of his arrest had caused her to have a miscarriage of his child.

"It isn't fair that you have everything now and I have nothing," she concluded, sobbing as she sagged between Andrew and Aaron's rather helpless support. "You're pretty and you live in a great place. Your family spoils you rotten. Now you've got a good-looking new man who's obviously crazy about you and you're going to have his baby—the very man who helped you send Wade away. You have everything, and you left me with nothing."

Steven looked out the broken window during the silence that followed Patricia's outburst while everyone struggled to understand her twisted reasoning. "A police car is turning into the drive. Someone should go out to greet them."

Patricia wailed even louder.

"Maybe we shouldn't press charges," Hannah said, looking at Andrew. "She certainly isn't the only woman who was taken in by Wade's lies. Heaven only knows what he told her."

Several in the room objected to Hannah's attempt at leniency, but Andrew spoke clearly over them. "We'll tell the police exactly what happened," he said implacably. "She slashed your tires, sabotaged your porch and barely missed hitting you with that rock. The latter is the only one we can prove, but it's an assault and she'll be charged for her crime."

"Seriously, Hannah, you'd let her go so she can come back and attack you again?" Maggie demanded. "You heard her, next time she'll throw a Molotov cocktail."

"I never want to see this place or any of you again," Patricia fervently assured them, her plain, tear-streaked face set in a hard expression.

C.J. escorted two uniformed officers into the room. Her heart heavy, Hannah fell mostly quiet then, except to give brief responses to the questions that were asked of her. Watching her family trying to clean up the damage to their home, and her grandmother sipping tea in an attempt to settle her nerves, she wondered just how much more distress her past mistakes would end up costing the ones she loved.

"That woman was truly delusional," Sarah said when Patricia Gibson had been taken away. "To think that she blamed Hannah—blamed all of us—for Wade going to jail, when it was his own greed and dishonesty that sent him there."

Andrew wasn't particularly surprised. In the course of his investigations, he'd heard too many women make too many excuses for badly behaving men.

He blamed himself for not even considering one of Wade's cast-off women as Hannah's stalker. He'd found evidence of the affairs, but his investigation had focused on finances, so he hadn't bothered to follow up on specific names. Especially because Wade hadn't trusted any of those women enough to partner with him in his crimes. Andrew doubted that Wade had considered his probably brief affair with Patricia to be the great romance she'd envisioned it.

Hannah, he noted, had become very quiet since Patricia was escorted away. He imagined she was tired, stressed. A little sad, perhaps, that another woman had been taken in by her ex. She was very carefully not meeting his eyes—not meeting anyone's eyes really, but she seemed to be avoiding him in particular. He wished he knew what she was thinking.

"That girl is just flat-out crazy as a Bessie bug," Pop pronounced flatly. "Believing all those lies Wade told. Saying Andrew is the father of Hannah's baby."

Andrew sensed that Maggie, Shelby and Aaron all shifted their weight or cleared their throats uncomfortably, probably wondering how Hannah would respond to that. Truth be told, he was curious about that himself.

With all eyes upon her, Hannah drew a deep breath and stood, one hand resting lightly at her middle. She was a bit pale, making the fresh scratches stand out against her skin, but her chin was high and her voice steady when she said, "No, Pop. Whatever other delusions Patricia suffers from, she wasn't wrong about that. Andrew is my daughter's father."

There was a moment of silence—stunned in the case of those who hadn't already known, expectant for those who had.

"I'm sorry, Mom, Dad," Hannah said. "I should have told you sooner. And don't blame Andrew that I didn't. I asked him not to say anything."

"Andrew is the baby's father?" Bryan looked bewildered as he studied both Hannah and Andrew in turn. Andrew moved to stand beside Hannah, close but not touching, offering moral support. "You mean, you two have been seeing each other since he left here last summer? But— When?"

"You don't need to know all the details," Hannah said firmly, making it very clear she had no intention of answering questions about the how and when—though at least part of the when was obvious, Andrew thought with a glance at her belly. "Just suffice it to say that Andrew is the father, and that he plans to be an active part of the baby's life. I hope you'll all respect our privacy and accept whatever decisions we make on our daughter's behalf."

Pop was the one to ask the question both Andrew and Hannah had expected, probably beating his wife to it by only seconds. "Does this mean y'all are getting married?"

"No, Pop, we aren't getting married." Again, Hannah's tone brooked no argument. "That's one of the decisions you're going to have to accept and respect."

Andrew bit his tongue. This wasn't the time for him to speak up, he reminded himself. That would wait until he and Hannah were alone.

"Humph," Pop grumbled beneath his breath, but just loud enough for the rest to hear. "Aaron's moved in with Shelby, Andrew's having a baby with Hannah. Doesn't seem like the Walker twins are the marrying kind."

Andrew bit down so hard on his tongue he almost tasted blood. He suspected his brother did the same. Their own family would have been in shock at the very suggestion that any Walker did not believe in the sanctity of marriage. Aaron and Shelby were only in their early stages of their romance—which, granted, was proceeding very swiftly—and Hannah wouldn't even discuss the possibility with him, so Pop was being a bit unfair to make such a sweeping statement.

Now that Linda had taken a moment to recover from her initial surprise, she didn't seem as startled by hearing about Hannah and him. Perhaps she had sensed the undercurrents between them, or maybe something they had said or done had given her pause. She looked at him and he searched for disapproval in her eyes but found none. "Have you told your parents yet?"

He shook his head. "We wanted to tell you first. I'll tell them when I go back to Dallas tomorrow."

Linda turned her attention to her daughter. "Are you going with him to talk to them?"

"No," Hannah replied. "He invited me, but that was before we knew Lori wouldn't be here to fill in for me while I was gone. With the holiday coming up, I'm needed here."

"We can manage if you want to go with him to talk to his family," Shelby insisted. "I can man the desk and still work on the books."

Hannah shook her head stubbornly. "That would add at least two hours a day to your work. I won't put you or anyone else in that bind. After everything that's happened here lately, we need to get back to normal. I intend to start working on that immediately."

She could cling as hard as she liked to her old "normal," but that wouldn't stop change from coming, Andrew thought privately. He understood why the events of the past few months had left her unsettled, anxious, worried about the future. But everything *had* changed and the sooner she acknowledged that, the better.

He felt someone take his arm, and he glanced down to find Shelby leaning companionably against him, smiling up at him with her usual warmth. "So, you're my niece's daddy. Welcome to the Bell family, Andrew."

He wasn't sure if he was more startled by hearing himself called "daddy" or by the implicit acknowledgment that his connection with Hannah and their child automatically meant this family would be a significant part of his life from here on out. Looking around the room, he decided he had no complaints about that.

Even though she knew many conversations would come, Hannah was relieved that the family didn't say much more that evening in response to her announcement. Mimi and Pop were tired, so C.J. and Sarah walked them home. After making sure the broken window was secured for the night, the others drifted off, too.

"You're sure you're okay?" her mom asked, touching her fingertips very lightly to the shallow cuts on Hannah's face.

"I'm fine, Mom," Hannah replied gently, giving her mother a quick hug. "And now that Patricia's gone, I'll be perfectly safe."

Her mother chuckled softly. "Oh, I'm sure Andrew would make sure of that anyway," she said, looking his way with affection and gratitude.

Hannah bit her lip, resisting an automatic urge to remind her mother that she could take care of herself. "We'll, um, talk tomorrow," she said instead. "Good night, Mom."

She kissed her father, then rushed Andrew outside before anything else could be said.

She noted that Andrew tested the railing on the porch when he escorted her home, giving it a good shake to make sure it held steady. He wasn't going to trust that railing anytime soon. She lifted an eyebrow. "My father is a very competent carpenter. He would make certain everything was solid before he put away his tools."

Andrew smiled a bit sheepishly. "I'm sure he would. Just needed to check again for myself."

As she'd expected, he followed her inside without waiting for an invitation. She tossed her keys on a table and turned to look at him. "You know, there's really no need for any of you to worry about me now. Patricia won't be back."

"I know. You should probably file a restraining order against her, just in case."

"Yes, I will."

"Aaron knows how to go about that if you need help with it after I leave," he fretted.

"Trust me, I know how to file a restraining order," she said, irked to hear the unintended hint of bitterness in her own tone.

After a moment, he nodded. "Yes, I suppose you do."

She sank to the couch, her hands clasped in her lap. She should probably offer tea or something, but she was just too wiped-out by the events of the day to make the effort.

Andrew sat beside her, covering her tightly gripped hands with one of his own. "Are you okay?"

"I'm tired," she replied candidly. "It's been a long day. A long week."

He nodded. "You should rest."

"I will. I think I'll turn in early tonight."

"Good plan. You're sure you won't come to Dallas with me? You could rest there while I'm at work. My place is comfortable, and there's a nice, cool patio with padded furniture where you can put your feet up and work from a laptop."

She had to admit it sounded tempting, especially when she thought of Andrew joining her on that patio for a cold iced tea after work. The image made her heart ache, which made her protective barriers snap into place again. She withdrew her hands from beneath his and shifted a few inches away from him on the couch.

"Sounds lovely," she said lightly, "but I really can't. Just as you need to be back in your office tomorrow, I need to be here."

She could tell that he wanted very badly to argue. She imagined that Andrew was unaccustomed to being turned down when he presented an argument so logically and persuasively.

"I'm disappointed," he said, sounding sincere, "but I'll accept your decision. Maybe you can come with me another time soon to meet my family."

She replied noncommittally, "Maybe."

"So, I'll be back next weekend. I'll stay in touch by phone in case you need anything. I'll leave all my contact information with you, though of course you can always reach me through Aaron, too."

She nodded, thinking that it would be unlikely that she would need to contact him in the next week, but it would be good to have the information anyway.

"When I get back, I'd like to continue the conversation we tried to have earlier," he continued. "About our options for the future. Maybe we'd rather do that in person than over the phone."

Remembering that he'd casually listed marriage as one of those options, she swallowed hard. "Yes."

As if he'd read her thoughts, he said, "I wish you would think about what I said. Marriage could be a good solution for us, both logistically and financially. It would allow us to raise our child together without worrying about visitation agreements and the problems inherent with long-distance parenting. I've got a nice apartment, but we could buy a house with a big back-yard for her to play in. You could continue to work as the marketing and scheduling director for the resort of course. You'd be only four hours away, so you could make the drive as often as you want or need to, though much of your work can be done online."

He had it all thought out, she mused dully. He might as well have read his talking points off a checklist. She lifted a hand to her temple, feeling a low throb begin there.

Andrew followed the movement with his eyes. "Do you have a headache?"

"Yes. Like I said, long day. It's nothing a good night's sleep won't fix."

"You should rest, then. Can I get you anything?"

She shook her head, relieved by the change of subject. "No, thank you. But I think I'll just turn in."

"Would you like me to stay with you? Just in case you feel worse later?"

"I'm sure I'll be asleep as soon as my head hits the pillow. You should go."

His expression inscrutable, Andrew nodded and stood. "I'll be right across the street if you need me."

Even though originally he'd planned to leave that evening, he'd decided to wait until morning to head out. Maybe he was tired from the chaotic events of the past couple of days, or maybe he was a little reluctant to leave. He hadn't said, and she hadn't been quite brave enough to ask, uncertain that she was prepared for his possible answer.

"I'll be fine on my own," she said.

He studied her face as if trying to decide whether those words held deeper meaning. "I'll see you in the morning before I leave," he said at length. "And I'll call you from Dallas."

She nodded.

"And you'll think about what I've suggested?"

She drew a breath. "We'll discuss many things when you get back, but you might as well know now that marriage is off the table. That's not an option."

"Don't just reject the idea out of hand. Take some time to think about it."

"That's not necessary." She rose then to fully face him. "I'm not interested in being married again. I was married before for all the wrong reasons, and I'm not going to go through that again."

A muscle jumped hard in Andrew's cheek. "You're comparing me to your ex-husband?"

"Of course not." She couldn't blame him for being insulted if he believed that. "You're nothing like Wade. Not in any way. But I'm still not going to marry just because I got pregnant. I prefer to remain single. As for our daughter, she'll have two large, loving families who will always put her best interests first. She won't lack for anything she needs."

"Hannah—"

She walked past him to open the door. "I really need for you to go now, Andrew. I'm very tired."

He studied her with narrowed eyes, then nodded. "We'll talk later."

She remained silent.

Andrew moved toward the door, pausing directly in front of her. Before she could prepare herself, he reached out to snag the back of her neck and plant a hard kiss on her lips.

"Get some sleep," he said gruffly when he released her.

As if that would be possible now, she thought as she closed the door behind him and leaned her throbbing forehead against it. She wished there was a pill she could safely take to soothe both her headache and her broken heart.

Chapter Ten

"Andrew, you big dummy."

In response to Shelby's disgusted condemnation immediately after he'd answered his phone, Andrew frowned in bewilderment. "What did I do?"

"For a very intelligent man, you can be such a dummy."

Standing on the rock patio of his parents' suburban Dallas home Monday evening after dinner, he drew a deep breath of warm night air and held on to his patience with an effort. "Okay, we've established that you think I'm a 'dummy.' Now, maybe you'd care to explain why?"

"Just how badly did you screw up your proposal to Hannah? You must have really made a mess of it."

He grimaced. "Hannah told you I proposed?"

"Well, no. I sort of guessed. She wouldn't even confirm whether you did or didn't, but you just let me know I was right. And you must have screwed it up big-time."

Shelby and her uncanny theories. Andrew shook his head, thinking that her family really should take her more seriously, as he and Aaron had learned to do. "Why do you say that?"

"I guessed because of the look on Hannah's face every time Mimi hints about her marrying you, which hasn't been as often as I expected, by the way. Someone must have ordered her not to nag, probably Aunt Linda. Anyway, I got the feeling that you did propose and that Hannah turned you down. Probably because you made a complete mess of it."

"I didn't propose," he almost growled, growing increasingly uncomfortable with her barrage of blame. "Well, not exactly. I just suggested to her that marriage should be an option we consider for the future. With the baby coming and all. I told her it made sense financially and, uh, logistically."

"Oh, my God."

Suddenly hearing his own words in his head, he frowned. Surely he hadn't worded it quite that awkwardly. "It sounds worse now than it did then."

"It would have to."

Going on the defensive, he said, "Not that this is any of your business really, but I would think you'd approve that I want to do the right thing by Hannah and the baby."

"Do the right thing? Oh, Andrew, you just keep making it worse." Despite the words, Shelby's tone had warmed and softened now, sounding almost pitying rather than critical. Which didn't make him feel any better.

"She made it clear that she wasn't interested in remarrying for any reason, practical or otherwise. She said she married for the wrong reasons before and didn't want to do it again. I have to respect that decision." He'd talked to Hannah that morning, he remembered glumly, having taken a few minutes out of an insanely busy morning just to hear her voice. Maybe he'd hoped to hear that she missed him, if only a little. Instead, she'd blithely assured him that she was doing very well, and that there was no need for him to hurry back to the resort.

"Think about it, Andrew. She was married to a man who lied to her, used her, ran around on her, obviously never loved her. Of course she doesn't want to be married next to a man who considers it a sound financial and logistical decision."

He cleared his throat. "Look, I know you have your cousin's best interests at heart, but I don't think she'd appreciate our talking about her this way. Suffice it to say that I suggested marriage, she shot me down—hard—so we'll just concentrate on working together in the future for our daughter's best interests. As Hannah pointed out Sunday evening, we'd appreciate the family's support and respect."

"Just think about the things I said, okay? And maybe ask yourself if finances and logistics were the only reasons you asked her. Oh, and by the way—" he heard her clear her throat before she added "—maybe you won't mention this call to Aaron? He, um, suggested I should probably mind my own business."

Despite that suggestion, Aaron would quite likely be highly amused that Shelby had contacted Andrew just to call him a "dummy." Twice.

Shaking his head, Andrew slipped his phone into his pants pocket, then turned to find his aunt Michelle

D'Alessandro standing behind him, two margarita glasses in her hands. Still pretty and deceptively fragile in her late fifties, his father's younger sister had always held a special place in his heart. He'd spent a lot of time with her growing up; Michelle and his mom, Taylor, had been best friends long before his parents had even met. He loved all his aunts, both by blood and marriage, but he and Michelle had a special bond.

"Your mom made her famous frozen strawberry margaritas for dessert," she said, approaching him with one of the frothy pink confections extended. A thin slice of lime decorated the sugar-encrusted rim of the glass. "I thought you might like one."

"Sounds good. Thanks."

Michelle and her husband, Tony, had joined Andrew, his parents and his uncle Joe and aunt Lauren for dinner. During the meal, Andrew had finally announced that he was soon to be a father. Responding to the seemingly million surprised questions that had followed, he'd told them about Hannah, about the events that had brought her into his life, about her family and the resort. After the initial shock, his family had accepted the news well.

Reassured that he would be active in his daughter's upbringing and that they would see her often, his parents seemed pleased to think of themselves as grandparents. Unlike Hannah's family, his didn't ask about the possibility of marriage—probably because they knew he'd have told them if such plans were in the works. Still, he had a feeling his mom would get around to asking in private. He wondered if his dad would feel compelled to remind him of all those pregnancy-prevention lectures he'd given his sons through the years.

"Your mom and Lauren are in there discussing possible grandmother nicknames," Michelle said with a smile. "The more Taylor thinks about it, the more excited she is by the thought of having a granddaughter. She knows how much fun I've had with my two grandsons and how besotted Joe and Lauren are with their little Madelyn."

Michelle and Tony's daughter Carly and her husband, Richard Prentiss, had two sons, Dexter and Liam. Cute kids; Andrew saw them often at family events. The third generation so far ranged from his cousin Brynn's eighteen-year-old son, Miles, to his cousin Casey's three-year-old daughter, Madelyn. Claire Elizabeth, as he was already starting to think of his daughter, would have plenty of playmates when the family gathered.

"I'm sorry for eavesdropping, but I couldn't help overhearing something you said when I came out," Michelle said as Andrew took a savoring sip of the tart, icy margarita. "Feel free to tell me to butt out, but did I hear you say you proposed to Hannah and she turned you down?"

After only a momentary hesitation, he nodded. Avoiding any mention of the word *logistics,* he gave a quick summary of the situation to his aunt. She listened intently, sipping her drink, asking no questions but seeming to understand.

When he finished, she slipped an arm beneath his and leaned her head companionably against his shoulder. "Andrew, did I ever tell you that I was once engaged before I met your uncle Tony? I was swept off my feet by the guy—Geoff—and I was convinced he adored me. He certainly told me often enough that he did."

"No, I haven't heard about Geoff. What happened?"

Looking out at the moon-bathed lawn beyond the patio fence, she sighed lightly. "Turned out he was much more interested in my adoptive parents' money than he was in me. He wanted a high-ranking position in my father's company and a guaranteed spot in Dallas society, and he thought marrying me would get him those things."

Orphaned very young, Michelle and her six siblings had been separated for almost twenty-five years. Several of the siblings—Andrew's father and his twin included—had spent years in foster care. Michelle had been adopted by a wealthy couple here in Dallas and the youngest, Lindsey, by a family in Little Rock, Arkansas. After the death of her adoptive parents, Michelle had been the one to initiate the search to bring the siblings back together, hiring private investigator Tony D'Alessandro to find them. By the time they'd all been happily reunited, Michelle and Tony had fallen in love and married.

"You said Hannah told you she doesn't want to be married for the wrong reasons," Michelle continued. "I can understand that."

"Yes, but your situation doesn't apply here. Hannah works for the family business, which is reasonably successful but hardly an empire. I make a good salary myself."

Michelle shook her head with a soft laugh. "No. Even though it sounds as though Hannah's ex wanted a large piece of her family business, I'm sure she knows *you* aren't after money. But she's been badly burned, and those scars take a long time to heal. Tony certainly had his work cut out for him when he courted me. As gun shy as I was, he had to convince me he wanted to marry me for the right reasons, not for the wrong ones."

"Tony was smart enough to know you were the real treasure."

She hugged his arm fondly. "That's very sweet, thank you. So, there are some questions I think you need to ask yourself before you talk to Hannah again. Don't answer me, but just think about them, okay?"

"What questions?"

She hardly hesitated to make a mental list before speaking. "First, do you really want to marry her or do you just think you should because of the baby? And if you do want to marry her, why? And finally, would you still want to marry her if she wasn't carrying your child? Your honest answers to those crucial questions should tell you whether you asked her for the right reasons."

"And if I did? And she still says no?"

His aunt reached up to pat his cheek. "Then she doesn't know a treasure when she sees one. I'm afraid that's just a risk you'll have to take, my darling."

She took a step backward. "And now we'd better go inside before my friend Taylor fusses at me for monopolizing all her son's time and attention when I'm sure she wants many more details about her grandbaby."

He turned with her toward the door. Just before entering the house, his aunt paused to glance up at him. "This Hannah, is she a treasure, Andrew?"

He kissed her cheek. "Yes, Aunt Michelle, she is."

She smiled. "Then maybe you should figure out the answers to those questions sooner rather than later."

* * *

Hannah pressed a hand to her aching back and looked in her fridge without enthusiasm Wednesday evening. She had little appetite but knew she needed to eat. It wasn't that she lacked food. On the pretext of making more than they could possibly eat themselves, her mother, aunt and grandmother had all dropped by with covered dishes during the past few days. Pasta salad, bean burritos, lasagna and homemade vegetable soup sat on the refrigerator shelves in covered plastic bowls. Not one of them appealed to her at the moment. With a sigh, she took out the pasta salad, primarily because she could eat it cold.

She ate at the kitchen table, doggedly chewing and swallowing the pasta, cheese cubes, cherry tomatoes and olives tossed in a balsamic vinaigrette. It was good, she supposed. Filling anyway, which was all that counted at the moment.

Her laptop lay open on the table beside her plate. She'd promised her grandmother she'd work on a gift registry for the baby shower, but she was having trouble concentrating. It made her a little uncomfortable to list things she wouldn't mind getting as gifts. Had she not worried that Mimi would probably just register for her, she might have skipped the task altogether.

Her phone lay beside the computer. Her gaze continued to be drawn to the dark, silent screen. It wasn't that she was expecting any calls exactly, but she had to admit she'd thought Andrew would check in with her today. She hadn't talked to him since a quick call from his office Monday morning, when he'd told her that he was crazy-busy and would probably not get back to the resort until Saturday at the earliest. She'd assured him she was fine and told him there was no need to come back so soon. They still had plenty of time to make all their plans.

Still, she'd thought he would call. How often had she even crossed his mind in the past couple of days? Was he annoyed with her for rejecting his suggestion—she refused to call his prosaic offer a proposal—of marriage? She was sure he thought it would be easier—logistically—if they lived in the same house, raising their daughter together when he wasn't busy with his work. Yet she doubted that he was heartbroken that she'd turned him down. Unsuccessful business propositions rarely led to broken hearts, she thought with an undercurrent of bitterness.

Her heart wasn't completely shattered either, she assured herself, giving up on the meal and carrying her plate to the sink. Okay, sure, she loved him. And maybe she had fantasized a little about a perfect future with him and their daughter, a happily ever after ending that seemed unlikely considering the circumstances. Maybe she wouldn't get over her disappointment exactly, but she would survive it. She was strong. Independent. Capable. She had her family, her daughter, her work. She and Andrew could be friends and partners in raising Claire Elizabeth, even with separate personal lives. And there would be no more sharing a bed for them, she told herself sternly. The best way to get past those wistful fantasies was to put them firmly behind her. She needed a clear head when it came to dealing with Andrew, and making love with him clouded her mind to a point that she couldn't even think clearly.

She brewed a cup of herbal tea, deciding to spend the remainder of the evening relaxing in front of the television with her laptop. She wasn't sure what was on tonight, but she could always stream one of her favorite feel-good movies. Maybe watching someone else's happy ending would cheer her before bedtime. She had just settled onto the couch with the teacup in one hand and the TV remote in the other when someone knocked on her door. It wasn't Maggie's usual four-rap knock.

Glancing at the clock, she saw that it was just after 8:00 p.m. Curious, she set her tea aside and crossed the room. A gasp escaped her when she opened the door. "Andrew?"

He frowned. "You didn't check first to see who it was?"

"I didn't think of it. What are you doing here?"

He shook his head. "After all that has happened here during the past month, you should start thinking more about security."

Her heart was beginning to slow to its normal pace, though she still wasn't quite over the surprise of finding him at her door. She planted her hands on her hips. "Did you drive four hours just to yell at me for answering my door?"

Making a face, he pushed a hand over his hair. "Sorry. No, that's not why I came."

She moved aside to allow him to enter, closing the door slowly behind him. "I thought you said you were swamped with work this week."

His expression turned rueful. "I had my administrative assistant shuffle some things again. She's threatening to quit."

"So why did you come?" she asked, genuinely perplexed.

He took a step closer to her, and something in his eyes

now made her heart start to pound again. "I realized—with a little help from a couple of wise women—that I've been a dummy. I wanted to try to rectify that."

Clasping her fingers in front of her, she frowned and moistened her lips. *Dummy* was not a word she'd heard Andrew use before. It sounded rather out of character now. "I don't understand."

"My aunt Michelle gave me some questions to think about before I talked to you again. I've given them a lot of consideration, and I wanted to share my answers with you. In person."

"Questions?" She was growing more confused by the minute. "What questions?"

While Andrew's tone had been light, his expression was very serious as he steadily met her eyes. "There were three actually. Do I want to marry you, or do I think I should just because of the baby? If I do want to marry you, why? And would I still want to marry you if you weren't carrying my child?"

"Oh." She swallowed hard. "Those are…big questions."

He took another step forward, never looking away from her. "Do you want to hear my answers?"

Her fingers were tangled so tightly she could feel them cramping, but was only distantly aware of the discomfort. "I think I should."

Taking her hands in his, he rubbed his thumbs gently over the backs of them, soothing the tensed muscles. "I want to marry you," he said, his voice low and deep. "Not because I think I should, but because I love you and I want to spend the rest of my life with you. And while the baby may be the reason I came to the resort last week, I would still want to marry you even if you weren't pregnant. I've thought of you every day since we were together in December, and not a day has gone by that I didn't want to call you or come see you. The only reason I held back was because I thought you wanted me to stay away. I don't know how much longer I could have resisted even if the baby hadn't given me an excuse to see you again."

She blinked rapidly, refusing to allow threatening tears to escape her eyes. "I don't know what to say," she admitted in a choked whisper.

He nodded, as if he'd expected that. "Do you believe me?"

She bit her lower lip before reluctantly confessing, "I want to."

Holding both her hands in his left, he raised his right hand to caress her cheek with the backs of his fingers. "It's hard for you to trust again, isn't it? You've heard all these promises before."

The tears pushed harder, but she forced them back. "Yes."

"You said you didn't want to marry again for the wrong reasons. I've just given you my reasons for asking. Now maybe you should ask yourself those same questions before you give me a final decision," he suggested. "I can take no for an answer if that's your ultimate choice. And I won't rush you. Take all the time you need to be sure. I just wanted you to know that I'm aware of how badly I mishandled my proposal before. I've been kicking myself ever since for not telling you that I love you."

She couldn't believe she was hearing these words tonight. That he was even here to say them. Her mind spun with emotions. Shock. Hope. Fear.

He wasn't Wade, she reminded herself. No two men could possibly be more different. Words like these did not come easily to Andrew, as they had to glib Wade. She couldn't imagine Andrew using them for any reason other than because he meant them.

She drew a deep breath and asked shakily, "What were those questions again?"

She felt his fingers tighten a little around hers, but he kept his tone gentle when he replied, "Do you want to marry me?"

It had taken a great deal of courage for Hannah to concede defeat in her marriage, to look beyond infatuation and wishful thinking and face reality. She'd called on all her strength to tell Wade that she wanted out. Now she had to call on that inner fortitude again to take what could well prove to be the biggest risk of her life when it came to her happiness.

"Yes," she said, the one syllable deceptively simple.

Andrew's hand twitched again, as if he'd started to tremble just a little. Just the possibility that she could make Andrew tremble made her throat tighten almost unbearably. Yet his gaze held hers without blinking. "Why?"

Her voice emerged sounding a little choked but steady. "Because I love you. And I want to make a life with you."

His face very close to hers now, he asked the final question. "Would you still want to marry me even if we weren't having a baby?"

She wrapped her arms around his neck. "If it's for the right reason, then yes. I would still want to marry you. Very much."

Pulling her nearer, he asked huskily, "Is loving you more than my own life the right reason?"

"Yes, Andrew," she whispered against his lips. "That's exactly the right reason."

Looking pleased that he'd finally gotten it right, he covered her mouth with his.

Epilogue

Four-week-old Claire Elizabeth Walker looked perfectly content to be passed from one adoring relative to another, graciously accepting their admiration as her due. Considering the size and closeness of both the child's maternal and paternal extended families, Hannah figured it was a good thing her daughter enjoyed attention.

This latest get-together was being held on the first Sunday afternoon in October at Mimi and Pop's house. The heavy rush of summer resort business was behind them now that school had started again, though they still had a steady stream of guests to keep them busy, especially on weekends. Her cousin Steven was the guest of honor for this gathering. Fully recovered from his broken leg and in the best shape of his life, he was leaving tomorrow to begin his training as a firefighter and emergency medical technician. The family would miss having him here at the resort every day, but they'd learned to adapt to the new changes life continued to bring them.

Absently twisting the two-month-old wedding band on her left hand, she looked around this group of people she loved so dearly. A glittering new diamond on her own left ring finger, Shelby held Claire, cooing down at the sleepy baby while Aaron hovered nearby. Still quite happy in his job with the resort, and fully accepted now as both an important part of the business and the family, he smiled besottedly at both his fiancée and his niece. Hannah figured it wouldn't be long before another new Bell-Walker was announced. Her parents hovered nearby, eager to get their hands on their granddaughter again, while Mimi called out instructions from the other side of the room for Shelby to be sure and support the baby's head and not to let her get too warm or too cold or too wet or too tired.

Her uncle C.J. and aunt Sarah were remaining close to Steven, spending as much time with him as possible before he left for his training. She knew it would be hard for them to see him off tomorrow. It was difficult enough for them that Lori had moved to California with the new husband everyone was still trying to get to know. Lori insisted she was deliriously happy in her marriage to footloose musician Zach. Her family was doing all they could to support her despite the distance she'd put between them. Still, they missed her deeply and hoped she would someday be close to them again, emotionally if not physically.

In another corner of the room, Pop was telling tall tales to Andrew, who listened patiently and with apparent interest to stories he'd probably heard before. Her heart warming as it always did when she looked at the kind, loving, generous man who was her husband and the devoted father of her child, Hannah thought again of how very fortunate she was to have him in her life. Her trust had been well-placed this time. He was totally committed to her and to Claire, putting them before everything else in his life, even the career to which he'd devoted so much of his adult life.

They lived in Dallas most of the time, but made the drive to the resort often to see her family and his brother. Hannah was getting back to work now that she'd fully recovered from childbirth, figuring out ways to handle her responsibilities through telecommuting while the baby slept nearby. Her mother-in-law, an advertising professional who was a senior partner in her own firm, had been quite beneficial in helping her set up. Hannah was already very fond of her in-laws, and was slowly learning the names of Andrew's many aunts, uncles and cousins.

Seeing her watching him, Andrew excused himself from her grandfather and crossed the room to her. He slipped an arm around her waist, which was much smaller than it had been a month before. She had a little way to go yet before she was back to her pre-pregnancy size, but she was being faithful to her exercises, wanting to be in good shape to chase a toddler around when Claire learned to walk.

"You think we'll ever get our hands on our daughter again?" Andrew asked, watching with a chuckle when Maggie swooped in to steal the baby from Shelby.

Hannah smiled. "When she gets hungry, they'll return her quickly enough." Their usually contented child was not one to suffer hunger quietly—at any hour of the day or night.

Still looking at their daughter, Andrew murmured, "She's a lucky little girl to have so many people who love her."

Hannah glanced up at him. "She's not the only lucky one."

Andrew grinned and brushed a kiss over her mouth, heedless of anyone who might see the show of affection. "No," he agreed, "she's not."

Sighing lightly, Hannah rested her head against his shoulder and beamed at the family milling through the room. She had never been this happy, she realized. Marrying Andrew had been the wisest decision she had ever made—for all the right reasons.

* * * * *

A sneaky peek at next month…

Cherish™

ROMANCE TO MELT THE HEART EVERY TIME

My wish list for next month's titles…

In stores from 21st June 2013:

☐ Falling for the Rebel Falcon – Lucy Gordon

& The Man Behind the Pinstripes – Melissa McClone

☐ Marriage for Her Baby – Raye Morgan

& The Making of a Princess – Teresa Carpenter

In stores from 5th July 2013:

☐ Marooned with the Maverick – Christine Rimmer

& Made in Texas! – Crystal Green

☐ Wish Upon a Matchmaker – Marie Ferrarella

& The Doctor and the Single Mum – Teresa Southwick

Available at WHSmith, Tesco, Asda, Eason, Amazon and Apple

Just can't wait?

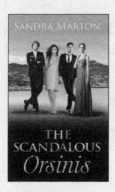

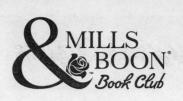

Join the Mills & Boon Book Club

Want to read more **Cherish**™ books?
We're offering you **2 more** absolutely **FREE**!

We'll also treat you to these fabulous extras:

- **Exclusive offers and much more!**
- **FREE home delivery**
- **FREE books and gifts with our special rewards scheme**

Get your free books now!

**visit www.millsandboon.co.uk/bookclub
or call Customer Relations on 020 8288 2888**